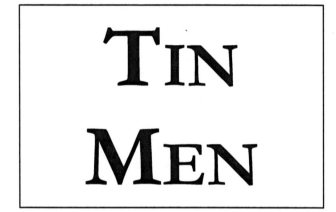

TIN MEN

Also by Amalie Jahn:

The Clay Lion
Among the Shrouded

Let Them Burn Cake!
(Available early 2015)

Amalie Jahn

TIN MEN

A NOVEL

ISBN-13: 978-0-9910713-1-9 (BERMLORD)
ISBN-10: 099107131X

Library of Congress Control Number: 2014912590
BERMLORD, Charlotte, North Carolina

First Edition, July 2014

Typeset in Garamond
Cover art by Amalie Jahn

To Drew-

The person who taught me what sacrifice, perseverance,
and true love are all about.
Thank you for being my real-life Charlie,
without all the loathsome sensitivity.

CHAPTER ONE

It was raining, but only barely. It was an in-between kind of rain. The type that can't decide if it wants to be a soft mist or a full-on drizzle. I held the umbrella above our heads as Brooke methodically marched in place to keep her heels from sinking into the soft earth. My mother stood beside me, sharing her umbrella with Melody. Hundreds of mourners surrounded us, including Brooke's parents and my extended family, but as far as I was concerned, we were the only four people on earth.

The minister was still speaking. I stopped listening to whatever he was saying about my father, his life, and the many outstanding contributions he left behind. His words meant nothing to me.

Brooke reached for my hand which I eagerly took. Her fingers were cold, as they always were, even in the middle of July. Her presence strengthened me as I watched my mother and sister blotting their eyes with shredded tissues. It was emotionally exhausting to see them in pain, and I was at a loss for how best to console them. Brooke had lost her only brother just before we met and had somehow managed to carry on despite the strong bond they shared. I squeezed her hand, and she peered up at me from behind her hair. I knew she was wondering why I was the only one who hadn't cried about my father's death.

The truth was, I had no tears to shed for the man who had been my father but never my dad. I knew she wanted me to mourn his loss, but the reality was, not much in my day to day life would change now

7

that he was gone. A trust fund would sustain me financially, and since my father had never supported me emotionally, my life would continue on in much the same manner as it always had.

As the service ended, we were encouraged to approach the mahogany casket to say our final goodbyes. I followed behind my weeping mother, who placed her hand upon the glossy surface. As she stepped away, Brooke gave me a gentle nudge and I took a step closer. I read the inscription on the side of the box – "Phillip Henry Johnson: Husband, Father, Public Servant." I closed my eyes and willed myself to feel something that resembled grief. Instead, I felt only indifference. I stepped aside to make way for the throng of constituents who dabbed bloodshot eyes and shook their heads in quiet disbelief.

As we made our way toward the waiting town car, Brooke broke the silence that had been looming over us for most of the day. "I'm worried about you," she said, her concern visible in the lines crinkling her forehead.

I smiled at her. "Don't worry. I'm fine. Life goes on, right?"

"It does," she frowned, "but usually not right away."

The rain stopped and I lowered the umbrella, shaking the water droplets onto the ground. I followed Brooke into the car, sliding across the back seat beside her.

"It's okay to be sad, you know?" she said, laying her head on my shoulder.

I didn't respond. I couldn't. Although Brooke and I had been inseparable since the day we met, there were still parts of my life she didn't understand. Her family was close. Loving. Supportive. Hers was the type of family Norman Rockwell had painted. Even her brother's death hadn't shaken their faith or love for one another.

My family was *not* that kind of family.

My father had been a politician and a politician above all else. During campaigns and elections, my father paraded us around, his perfect nuclear family for the world to praise and admire. What the voters weren't aware of was in 20 years, he had never seen me swim the final leg of a medley relay. They didn't see the empty seat at the kitchen table during mealtimes. And they certainly didn't realize he never showed affection unless cameras were rolling to capture the moment. The Phil Johnson the world knew was not the Phil Johnson that Melody and I had for a father. And so, instead of sadness, I felt only regret that my father had squandered his time with us.

"I can't go to the reception. I can't pretend for all those people. I know my mom wants me to be there, but I just don't think I have it in me."

She nodded supportively. "I know it's been hard. Is there something else you want to do? Somewhere you want to go?"

I brushed a lock of hair from across her face. I didn't say it, but I was already where I wanted to be. Anywhere with her, the most grounded, solid woman I knew, was right where I belonged.

"Let's just go to my house," I said. "Watch a movie. Order a pizza. Forget that I'm supposed to be the heartbroken Senator's son."

She took my hand. "You got it."

CHAPTER TWO

"I've been looking for you for half an hour," Brooke said, with only a hint of exasperation in her voice as she peeked through the doorway into my father's study. She walked across the room and sat behind me on the floor, wrapping her arms around my waist. "Your mom and Melody just got here. I ordered pizzas and they're on the way. I even got your favorite, ham and pineapple."

When I didn't immediately respond, she maneuvered beside me, raising an eyebrow in my direction. "Don't tell me you're not hungry. You're always hungry."

"It's not that," I replied at last, coming out of a daze, "it's all this."

Somehow I became absorbed in my father's belongings, which were spread across the ornamental rug in the center of the room. When I passed by the door to the office, a door that was never open and frequently locked, something made me hesitate and try the knob. To my surprise, it opened. I rushed inside, peering over my shoulder, as if my father had the power to return from the grave to admonish me, as he'd done my entire life.

Once inside, I wandered around for several moments, looking for something to prove once and for all that my father had loved me. A photograph of us together. A cherished coloring page from my youth. Something. Anything.

What I found instead was the box of gear the police department returned to my mother after completing the autopsy.

"These are the ropes he was wearing when he fell," I said, holding up a section of my father's climbing gear.

Brooke held the rope in her hand as if it was a venomous snake.

"I was never allowed in here, you know. Before. When he was alive. So I thought maybe, if I spent some time with his things, it would make me feel something."

"And?" she asked, tossing the rope on the floor and picking up a loose carabiner.

"And, no. It's just stuff." I paused, considering whether to go on. "But there is something strange I noticed."

"What's that?"

"This rigging," I said, holding up a twisted lump, "has fallen apart. And what's still together is all wrong. My father would have never tied it this way. It's not safe."

"Maybe it got messed up by the police during the cleanup after the accident," she suggested.

I had already considered that explanation, and concluded the disastrous ropes weren't the product of a sloppy investigation. And yet, it was unlike my perfectionist father to tie his anchor in such a dangerous way.

"Do you see this rope here?" I said, holding out the length in question. "This is an anchor. It's designed to hook onto the belay, which keeps you from falling in case you slip while you're climbing. But this anchor is tied all wrong, and it appears to have been done this way on purpose. My father always kept his fittings tied from one climb to the next. He never undid them. But I've never seen him tie an anchor this way." I inspected the ropes and realized the magnitude of the mistake. "See how the carabiners are hooked to three sides of the anchor making a sort of triangle shape?"

"Yeah. What's wrong with that?"

"What's wrong with that is the way this is tied, if one of these corners fails, they all fail. The whole anchor falls apart. That's probably what happened to the one that's pulled apart."

Brooke was silent for several moments before speaking. "What are you thinking, Charlie?"

I shook my head. I was reeling. Had my father suffered a momentary lapse in judgment when tying his anchor? Had he simply made a mistake? A mistake that led to a 100-foot fall and his own death?

"I don't know what to think," I sighed, picking myself up off the floor. "I guess I'll just pack this stuff back up and then we can have some pizza."

Brooke wandered around the study while I tucked the ropes and climbing gear back into the box. I was glad she was there. My Brooke. The woman who stole my heart and soul in one fell swoop. I never believed in love at first sight until I saw her across the quad, tossing a football with my friends in the fall of my sophomore year. Before I met her, I'd been afraid to love. Afraid to allow anyone behind my carefully constructed wall. A wall I created because I was afraid of being cast aside. But I felt, in that moment, she was someone I could take a chance on letting into my life.

As I watched her from across the room, nosing through my father's desk, I felt at ease for the first time in days.

"You ready?" I asked as I snapped the lid onto the box.

"Yeah, I guess. But Charlie?" She hesitated, glancing up at me with the look of a four-year-old who was caught with her hand in the cookie jar. "Who's this?" she asked finally, holding out a piece of paper in her hand.

"What is that?"

"It's an old photo. It was here," she said, "in your father's desk drawer."

She crossed the room and handed me the picture.

The woman in the photograph was beautiful. A graceful wisp of a woman, staring into the distance instead of looking into the camera. It was obvious she was been unaware she was being photographed, and that whoever took the picture had done so from afar. The woman was someone I didn't know. And yet, I saw her face every day of my life.

"She looks a lot like you, Charlie," Brooke whispered.

It was true. She had my eyes. My nose. My pronounced

cheekbones. Or rather, I had hers.

I attempted to steady myself on the corner of the desk, but my legs could not support my weight. Like an accordion, I crumpled to the floor, and in an instant, Brooke was there, in my lap, holding my head in her arms. As I struggled to breathe, she ran her fingers through my hair and whispered into my ear.

"It's okay. It's going to be okay," she repeated until her soothing became something of a mantra.

The truth was I always knew this woman existed. Somewhere, in the deepest recesses of my mind, I always knew that my mom hadn't given birth to me. She and I looked nothing alike, especially as compared to Melody, who could have passed for her sister. But there was more to it than just appearance. Through the years, there had been many heated conversations between my parents which shifted into silent standoffs as soon as I entered the room. I overheard them discussing monetary transactions and a woman who I "didn't need to know about." When I asked questions, they told me to mind my own business. When I snooped, I found only locked doors and empty files. My parents kept a secret from me my entire life. And it was finally time to find out the truth.

CHAPTER THREE

"I don't know if now is the best time to have this conversation with your mom, Charlie," Brooke said when I finally composed myself and was heading for the door.

"She's had my entire life to discuss this with me!" I spat, unable to control the anger bubbling up inside of me. "But she always sided with my father. She never told me the truth." I turned to face Brooke as I stood in the doorway. "She's going to tell me the truth today."

I headed down the hall and she rushed to my side. "She's reeling, Charlie! His death may not be affecting you, but it's affecting her." She grabbed my hand and held her ground at the top of the staircase. "Don't do this to her. She's your mom. Have some compassion."

I looked into her eyes. I swore when I looked into them there were times I could see her soul. It was an old soul. A soul that knew more than someone her age should know. And I knew she was right about my mom. She was always right when it came to knowing the right thing to say and the reasonable thing to do. But in that moment, I didn't care about doing the right thing. I only cared about the truth.

"Come with me. Tell me what to say so I don't hurt her feelings. But please, Brooke, please, don't tell me not to ask her for the truth."

She considered me for several seconds, and I could see her reassessing her position. Still gripping my hand, she turned on her heel and led me down the stairs. We found my mom and Melody sitting at the kitchen island eating pepperoni pizza off paper plates.

When I saw her, my resolve wavered. I knew without a shadow

of a doubt that she had not given birth to me. I knew I was adopted. But I also knew she was the woman who had seen me through the chicken pox and two broken arms. The one who packed my lunches for 13 years and folded all my laundry. She'd been to every swim meet and soccer game. She had never treated me as anything other than her son. I knew what I was about to say was going to hurt her. And yet, I knew I couldn't let another day go by without knowing why they never told me the truth.

"Charlie, what is it?" she asked, when I didn't join her at the counter. "Don't you want something to eat? We have..."

"Ham and pineapple," I interrupted. "I know. Thank you."

I sat down beside her and took a slice of pizza from the box, but laid it on a plate without taking a bite. I looked at Brooke, who was standing across the counter from me, waiting. I inhaled deeply through my nose and released the air slowly through my teeth.

"Mom," I began, "now that it's just us. Just me and you and Melody, there's something I need to ask you."

I heard the sound of her breath catch in her throat. She let the slice of pizza slide from her hand onto the counter. She didn't look at me. I don't think she could have even if she wanted to. She didn't speak.

She knew.

"Mom..." I started again, fumbling for words. I looked to Brooke, begging her with my eyes for assistance.

"Mrs. Johnson," she said, "Charlie believes his father kept something important from him while he was alive. And well, now that he's no longer here, he would like to know the truth from you, if you'd like to share it with him. But if now's not a good time..."

I touched my mom's shoulder, afraid she would withdraw, but she didn't. Instead, she turned to face me, tears in her eyes and a crooked smile on her face. She shook her head.

"For over twenty years I've kept your father's secret. I never understood why it was so important to keep the truth from you, but he never wanted to give the public any reason to question him. I don't know how anyone could view what he did in a negative light, but he never wanted anyone to know, just the same. I guess now that he's gone, it doesn't make much of a difference either way. He was a good man," she said, patting my hand. "Maybe hearing the truth will help you see that."

"What truth, Mom?" I asked, uncertain if I was ready to hear the words I knew were coming.

Without answering, she crossed to the far side of the kitchen, where she selected a bottle of red wine from the rack. After pouring herself a sizable glass, she made her way into the family room where she settled herself on the oversized sectional and waited patiently for us to join her. After several anxious moments, she finally spoke.

"Phil and I had been dating for just about a year. He had recently proposed, and things were going so well between us that I couldn't imagine life being any more perfect. He was running for county commissioner, a position he was sure would lead to bigger and better things in the future, and he was ahead in all the polls. He was sure he had the nomination locked up and was on cloud nine. I don't remember ever seeing him more excited than he was during that election. Then one evening, he called me out of the blue and said he needed to speak with me right away. I wasn't expecting to see him that night because he was attending some sort of charity event, but he was adamant about a face-to-face conversation.

"I met him at the Box Car Diner. You know the one in Bakersville, just off route 52? I ordered a slice of key lime pie, but all he ordered was a cup of coffee." She paused. "I never did eat my pie."

My mother sat sipping her wine for several minutes as if she forgot she was involved in a conversation with the rest of us. It was as if she was no longer in the room, but had instead been transported back to the night she was describing. For some reason, she was hesitant to go on.

"Mom?" I said. "What did he tell you?"

She blinked twice as if to refocus her attention on the present and continued.

17

"He told me a woman visited him that afternoon who said she'd gotten pregnant and given birth to a baby boy. She claimed that the child was his. He assured me it was impossible, and that he'd never met the woman before in his life. Phil was beside himself with worry that she would ruin his career with her lies, just as he was finally beginning to make a name for himself in the political world. The worst part, he said, was that she was strung out on God knows what kind of drugs. It was obvious to him she had no business raising a child."

She took another sip of wine and stared straight ahead, as if she could no longer bring herself to look in my direction. Finally, she began again.

"Phil was always a kind man. A generous man. A giving man. The decision he made about that woman erased any doubts I had about whether I wanted to spend the rest of my life with him."

As she turned to look at me, pain chiseled the lines of her face. I knew what she was about to confess.

"Charlie, my sweet Charlie. I didn't give birth to you, but you should know that you have always been my son. Phil couldn't stand the thought of such a deplorable woman raising you. After several medical professionals examined her, they deemed her unfit to parent. If I remember correctly, she was admitted to some sort of rehabilitation clinic. The authorities were unable to locate your father, and since there was no other family willing to take you in, you became a ward of the state. We began the adoption process immediately." She sighed, deflating like a week-old balloon. "I don't know why he never wanted to tell you, but there it is. That's the truth. And I love you. I've loved you since the first time I held your little hand in mine."

I closed my eyes to keep from passing out or throwing up. Brooke grabbed my leg, a supportive gesture. As the room continued to spin, I knew it would take more than her kindness to help me sort through my emotions.

I knew deep down I was adopted for as long as I could remember. But surprisingly, having the proof I so desperately wanted felt more like a prison sentence than a stay of execution. Instead of feeling complete, like a puzzle whose final piece had at last been put in place, a void opened up inside of me. Like a sink hole, which had been there all along under the façade of solid ground, there was now nothing but a gaping pit. And that pit was filled with anger and rejection and sadness.

I steadied myself and stood up from the sofa.

Mom rushed to console me. "I'm so sorry we didn't tell you before, while he was still alive. I'm so sorry you'll never have the opportunity to thank Phil for what he did for you."

Her words serrated the jagged edges of my gaping wound.

"Thank him?" I jeered. "Thank him for what? For lying to me for 20 years? For never thinking my need for the truth was more important than his need for control? It was always about his stupid career! Always! Not telling me meant he would never have to explain where I came from to anyone else which made things clean and simple, just the way he liked it. Only now, it's not clean and simple! Now it's a mess. How convenient he's not here to deal with it!"

"That's not fair, Charlie!" she cried out behind me as I stormed into the foyer and headed upstairs, taking the steps two at a time.

I slammed my bedroom door behind me and relished the sound of it echoing through the house.

I was angry at my father for lying to me. Angry that he took me from my birth mother all those years ago. I was angry that he put the demands of his career above my needs, and angry at Mom for going along with it. I was disappointed my sister wasn't really my sister, and that the family I believed in a week ago was nothing more than a charade. And I was angry my father wasn't even around so I could tell him just how angry I was.

I threw myself across my bed and beat my fists into the mattress, but it wasn't enough to release the wound up rage inside me. I needed to throw something. Anything. I picked up a large swimming trophy from my bookshelf, one of the many my father hadn't seen me earn. I positioned myself to launch it at the wall. But just before my hand released, a vision of my mom beaming at me from across the pool deck flashed before my eyes. She was as proud of me that day as any parent would have been of their own flesh and blood, cheering me on from the sidelines meet after meet.

I returned the trophy to my desk and instead began to pace, from my bed to the window and back again.

As I continued to pace the length of my room, waiting for Brooke or Melody or Mom to make an appearance, my fury began to subside. I realized I was as angry with myself as I was with anyone else.

I knew the woman in the photo was my mother the moment Brooke showed her to me. Yet for some reason I couldn't explain, I needed to hear the truth spoken aloud. And so because of my selfishness, I caused my mom additional, unnecessary pain on top of the devastation caused by my father's tragic death. Perhaps I was more Phil Johnson's son than I cared to admit.

As I collapsed onto my bed for a second time, there was a quiet knock at the door. When I didn't respond, Brooke let herself in.

She stood silently above me with her hands on her hips and a disapproving look on her face.

"Seriously, Charlie?" she scolded.

I sat up and scooted over to give her room to sit beside me, but she remained standing.

"I know. I'm acting like a child. But since I just found out I have *two* mothers, I certainly don't need a third."

She rolled her eyes. "I'm not trying to be your mother, Charlie. Especially since you already have an amazing one downstairs, in tears, struggling with how to convince you that becoming your mom was the best thing that ever happened to her. I just thought you should know." She glared at me before turning back toward the door.

A lump formed in my throat. "Is that what she said?"

"Yes. That's what she said."

I hesitated, considering her declaration.

"She thinks I should be grateful for what he did. For taking me away from my mother and giving me this life instead."

"Maybe you should be grateful."

The truth stung, especially hearing it from Brooke, whose insights were usually spot on. "I probably should. She's right. But it was just like him to do something like that. He always assumed he was right about everything. That he knew what was best for everyone." I was seething. "I hated that about him."

Brooke stepped back into the room, and as she sidled up beside me on the bed, her demeanor completely changed. She brushed my tousled hair aside and kissed me tenderly on the forehead. "Okay. You hated that about him. What else?"

"What else, what?"

"What else did you hate?"

I chuckled. "You want the whole list?"

"Yeah. The whole list. Give it to me."

I thought for a moment. "I hated that he loved the power of his job more than he loved me."

"Great. What else?"

I stood up. "I hated that he paraded us around like show ponies and snowed everyone into believing he was a great dad. And I hated the way he always expected me to want to be just like him and got angry when I didn't want to be anything like him. And most of all, I hated how he gave us the best of everything... but never the best of himself."

My vision blurred and I bit my lip in an attempt to stifle my emotions. Brooke joined me in the center of the room and folded herself into the space between my arms.

"It's okay to cry," she whispered.

Tears were already on their way, with or without her permission. The tears she'd been waiting to see since the news of my father's death finally arrived.

"He was a horrible father, but he was the only one I had, and now he's gone and it doesn't even matter because he wasn't even my father after all." I scrunched my face to keep her from seeing my pain.

"And the worst part is, you can't even tell him how mad you are about any of it," she finished for me.

I rested my chin on her head and pulled her into my chest. It was just like her to know how to express exactly what I was feeling before I knew I was feeling it. It was one of the many things I loved about her.

From the moment I met her, Brooke seemed to have known me, sometimes better than I knew myself. It was as if she'd always been a part of my life. Ever since the beautiful September afternoon when she pass rushed her way into my heart, she blended herself seamlessly into my life. In the months and years that followed, there were many times I felt as if I was still getting to know her, while she seemed to understand all there was to know about me. As unnerving as it could have been, I found there was great comfort in her faithful understanding, especially given the lack of emotional support I received from my father.

I took several deep breaths, allowing the familiar scent of her shampoo to soothe me. I didn't want to ever let her go.

"What do I do now?" I asked.

She hesitated, releasing herself from my embrace. "Is that a rhetorical question, or are you looking for an answer?"

"Both," I replied.

She picked up a football from beneath my desk and threw it at my head. I caught it.

"That's what you do," she said.

"I catch a football?"

"No. You react. You roll with the punches. You let this all play out, and when something gets chucked at your head, you deal with it."

"That's easy for you to say, Miss 'One with the Universe.' You always have your stuff together. Your brother died and you sailed right through." She caught the football I threw at her chest.

"I didn't, Charlie. I was a mess. It took me a long time to make peace with what happened. You have no idea how I fought. I beat my head against the wall. I swam against the tide. Until I decided to let it be."

"I don't know how to 'let it be,'" I confessed. "Or if I want to."

She threw the football at my head again.

"So if you're not ready to let it be, what do you want to *do*?"

I thought about her question. There were lots of things I wanted to do and a few that just couldn't wait, starting with mending my family's hurt feelings.

"I need to talk to Mom and Melody. I need to tell them we're going to be okay."

"*Are* you going to be okay?"

Yes. We had to be. They were my family, and I wasn't going to risk losing them.

"My mom will always be my mom and my sister will always be my sister. I love them. That hasn't changed, has it?"

"No, Charlie. How could it?"

"What if I did something that might hurt them?"

"Why would you do that?" she asked scornfully.

"It wouldn't be on purpose, but there's something else I want to do, Brooke. And it might make them sad." I hesitated to go on, knowing once the words were spoken aloud, I'd be unable to take them back. "I want to find my mother. My birth mother. Because if I can find her, then maybe I can stop feeling so lost. Mom said I was two when I was taken away. I must have missed her. I must have loved her. So perhaps if she can tell me the story of who I was when I was with her, then maybe it will help me make sense of who I am, since being adopted is part of my identity now. I just have to figure out if I'm going to allow it to shape the man I'm supposed to become."

Chapter Four

By the time I found the courage to approach Mom about finding my birth mother, both she and Melody had already gone to bed. I decided not to wake her, and instead curled up with Brooke on the living room sofa in front of the TV. I didn't remember falling asleep and was disappointed to find myself alone, still dressed in the suit pants I wore to the cemetery the day before, as the sun rose the next morning. At some point during the night, Brooke crept silently from my arms and went home, leaving me with nothing but the festering wound of my newly discovered family secrets.

I readied myself for the day, tormented by an onslaught of conflicting emotions. In addition to the pain of being lied to and the anger it produced, there was also a hollowness in my gut and an aching in my heart I wasn't expecting. I tried focusing on the anger because it was easier than acknowledging the rest, but the quiet grief of not knowing my biological family kept floating to the surface. It was as if I'd been stripped of a piece of my identity and was no longer exactly who I was before. As I tied my sneakers, I considered how finding my mother might help me regain my bearings and get me back on solid ground.

Thankfully, Mom and Melody were still asleep as I snuck out of the house. The confidence I mustered the night before disappeared with the dawn, and I lacked the courage to face them. I knew I needed more time to pull myself together if I was going to tell them about my plans. I was fearful about how they might react and knew the last thing

I wanted was to upset them. I had no idea whether they would support me in the search for my mother, or whether my intentions would drive an unintended wedge between us. And frankly, I was too scared to find out.

I drove aimlessly for almost an hour, ending up at the one place which always felt like home. As I pulled my car into Brooke's driveway, I realized it was not yet 7 o'clock. I rolled the windows down and closed my eyes, listening to the birds waking up in the forest. Several minutes passed, and I had just decided to head back home when I noticed Brooke's mother walking across the lawn in my direction.

I wasn't shocked to see her coming out to check on me. I still remembered the first time Brooke invited me to meet her parents. It was fall break, only five or six weeks after we first met. Having spent almost every waking moment together at school, the thought of being apart during break was unbearable to both of us. Brooke insisted we eat dinner together at her family's house that very first night. She promised her family would love me. She just felt it in her bones. And not surprisingly, she was right.

I became a regular fixture at the Wallace house throughout the years. I assumed her parents enjoyed having me around because I helped fill some of the void left by Branson's death, although Brooke assured me her family would have been just as welcoming if Branson had still been alive. In any case, Mrs. Wallace was something of a mother figure to me as well, so it wasn't strange to see her padding out to me in her robe and slippers, a coffee mug in her hand.

"Rough night?" she asked sympathetically as she approached the driver's side door.

"You could say that," I replied.

"Brooke told me a little bit when she got home last night." She shook her head. "I don't know why I still wait up for her, but I do. After her car accident in high school, I just need to know she's safe, I guess."

"That's understandable," I fumbled, embarrassed by how much

Brooke may have told her about my behavior the night before.

There was nothing to suggest she was bothered by my early arrival as she invited me to come inside. "I kind of had a feeling I'd be seeing you this morning. Don't know what you're doing sitting out here in the car. Come on inside. I made a fresh pot," she said, lifting her mug.

"Is Brooke awake?" I asked as I climbed out of the car.

"No. You can wake her if you want though. She won't mind."

I followed her into the kitchen with no intention of waking Brooke. However, as nice as her mom was, I also didn't plan on making small talk with her for the next hour. I was suddenly angry at myself for not thinking through my morning more carefully, but before I had a chance to think of a reason to leave, she pulled out a kitchen chair and placed a mug of coffee on the table.

"Milk and sugar?" she asked.

"Yes, please," I sighed, resigning myself to the chair.

There was a moment of silence as we sipped from our cups. She looked at me from across the table with a sympathetic smile as she began to speak.

"You know, Charlie, being a mom is a funny thing. You think you know how it's going to be before you have children. You think you know what love is. What it means to really, truly love someone. Like the love you have for Brooke. It's pure. Honest. Strong. But I promise you, it won't compare with the love you will feel for a child."

I didn't speak. I didn't know if she wanted me to acknowledge what she was saying was true or if she was merely talking to make herself feel better about my situation. She continued without waiting for me to respond.

"When you have a child, you give yourself to them. You allow that child to carry a piece of you around everywhere they go. It's not a conscious decision, it just happens. It's the way mothers are wired. When you are a mother, tasked with the greatest responsibility in the world, that of raising a tiny human into adulthood, you give your heart to that child, whether you want to or not. And the things you do for them, the everyday things, like teaching them to tie their shoes or signing up for the PTA bake sale or driving 45 minutes out of your way to deliver a forgotten homework assignment… those are the things you do out of love. Because your heart is out there in the world and it needs you.

"Charlie, your mom isn't your mom because she had to be. She's your mom because she wanted to be. She chose to be your mom every day for the past 20 years. She chose to give you a piece of her heart and let you walk around with it. She didn't have to, but she did. In my book, that's an even greater love than the love I have for Brooke and Branson because Charlie, she *chose* to love you. I didn't have that choice. She did. And she chose you."

I didn't know what to say. She was right, of course. I couldn't have wished for a more amazing mom than the one I already had. And yet I couldn't stop thinking about the mother I left behind.

"What about my birth mother?" I asked. "Do you think she loved me that way too?"

She was silent for a moment, studying my face. I could tell she was choosing her words carefully. "When you lose a child, you don't stop loving him. I know that for a fact. I don't know the circumstances surrounding your adoption, and I don't know what your life with her was like before you were adopted. But I would think that you are probably still carrying around a little piece of her heart."

I felt a pair of arms around my neck.

"Good morning, Sunshine," Brooke said, placing a kiss on my cheek.

"Hey," I replied, grateful for her arrival and immediately calmed by her presence. "You left last night."

"I know," she said, sliding into the chair beside me and giving her mother a knowing look across the table. Mrs. Wallace quickly got up, patted me on the shoulder, and left the room.

"I had to, Charlie," she began again. "You needed to be alone with your family and I didn't belong there. You need to work this out together, without me around."

"You're my family as much as they are," I retorted, unable to

28

silence the hurt.

"They are still your family, Charlie. Your parents did what they thought was best for you and..."

"My father did what he thought was best for him," I interrupted.

"You don't know that. You don't know what he was protecting you from all these years."

I frowned at her. "Whose side are you on?" I asked, anger boiling to the surface once again.

She reached across the space between us and took my hands. "I'm not on anyone's side. There are no sides. Just the truth and how you choose to react to that truth. I'm here though. On your team. Right beside you for as long as it takes to get through this."

"Maybe I'll never get through it," I sighed.

"Then I guess I'm stuck with grumpy-old you," she groaned, feigning exasperation. Then she smiled, a hint of laughter dancing in her eyes. I couldn't help but smile back.

"Maybe I'll let this thing drag out forever then, just to string you along, as long as you're making promises about staying with me."

"I can't let you do that. You need to move on." She paused. "How about if I promise to move on with you?" She climbed into my lap, her legs straddling my waist. The kitchen chair creaked beneath our weight.

I held her face in my hands and kissed her softly before wiping sleep from the corner of her eye. I rested my chin on the top of her head as she laid it on my chest. "I'm going to find my mother. I'm going to find out her side of the story, and you can help me react to whatever I find. But I can't move on until I know where she is and what happened to her. What happened to us. I need to know her story because it's part of my story too. Can we do that? Together?"

She picked up her head and looked at me seriously, the way she did whenever she had something important to say that needed to be heard. "We can do that. And I know just where to start."

After breakfast with her parents, Brooke and I headed to the local branch of the public library. Neither of us had to work until later in the day, so we intended to spend the morning searching for my mother.

"I don't know what you think we're going to find here," I said cynically as we pulled into the parking lot.

"I have some history with researching old files here. Everything isn't completely digital yet. There are still some paper files and I know how to find them. Just trust me."

I wondered what sort of information she researched in the past but decided not to ask. It was a Saturday morning, and the library was full of summer school students, parents with small children, and elderly men looking for peace and quiet. She headed straight for the circulation desk and began speaking enthusiastically with the librarian. I held back, wandering through the closest shelves, grateful to her for taking the lead. I was afraid of letting my anger, which I was holding at bay just beneath the surface, come out in such a public place. Additionally, I didn't have the faintest idea where to begin searching for my mother.

I was flipping through a book on WWII submarines when she appeared by my side, grabbing me by the arm.

"Come on! Let's go downstairs."

"I didn't even know this place had a downstairs."

"Stick with me, kid," she said in her best gangster voice as we entered the stairwell.

She skipped down the stairs in front of me, her hair bouncing off her shoulders, carefree as a child. Sometimes, that's how I saw her, as a woman-child, seemingly trapped between two worlds. I knew losing her brother at such a young age forced her to grow up before it was time. His death aged her prematurely. I watched her struggle to fit in with our lighthearted classmates, knowing she could never go back to regain the innocence the others still enjoyed. And yet, watching her skip joyfully down the stairs, I was able to catch a glimpse of the girl she had been before I met her. The girl she might still be if not for Branson's death.

"What are you waiting for?" she called as she reached the bottom of the stairs and headed down a corridor to our left.

I found her in a room the size of a large janitor's closet. There was a small table in the center and the walls were lined with metal file cabinets. There was an unusual machine on the table.

"What the heck is that?"

"It's called a microfiche machine. Before the internet, there was no mass digital storage but keeping actual paperwork took up too much space. So they had these instead," she said, holding up a transparent piece of plastic. "A lot of towns still keep public records on them as back up, just in case. Ours is one of them."

"So why aren't we just looking online?"

"Because the internet can be tampered with. It's full of information that's wrong. And some municipalities don't post personal information like we're looking for online. At least using this we'll know what we find is correct."

"Okay." I sat down in front of the machine. "So what are we looking for?"

"Your original birth certificate, of course. I assume on the one you have now, you're listed as Charles Johnson and your mom and dad are listed as your parents?"

She was brilliant. My birth certificate was the perfect place to start, and I would have never thought to look for anything beyond the one I already had. Of course, Phil and Karen Johnson were listed as my parents on the one I always used, but the original documentation would list my birth parents. I stood up, crossed the room in two strides and grabbed her by the shoulders to plant a kiss firmly on her lips.

"What's that for?" she asked when I finally allowed her to come up for air.

"That's because you are a regular Sherlock Holmes! My very own detective!" I laughed. "I guess that makes me Watson."

"Slow down, Doctor! We haven't found anything yet. This is just a place to start. We might not be able to find anything. We don't even know if your birthdate is your actual birthday. If you know the right channels and are motivated enough, it wouldn't be that tough to falsify."

I returned to the chair in front of the archaic piece of equipment. "How in the world do you know about this stuff?"

"I dunno. Guess I just get ideas. I like to solve problems."

Every time I thought I had Brooke Wallace figured out, I found something else to love. I kept waiting for the attraction to fade, the way it had with the girls I dated before her. But I found as time went by, there was more to love, not less. Not that we didn't have our occasional disagreements. And there were, of course, things she did that drove me crazy. Like refusing to drive more than one mile over the speed limit. It took us forever to get anywhere when she drove. I solved the problem by taking us wherever we needed to go. She was great with directions, so it all worked out.

I watched her scanning files in the drawers of the cabinets. "What exactly are you looking for?" I asked, feeling helpless. "Can I help search?"

"Sure. We're looking for all the birth certificates for baby boys born in April and May of the year you were born. Why don't you take a look in this section and see what you can find. It will be listed under the state's vital records."

We sat together for almost an hour, searching through manila envelopes and file folders. Finally, mercifully, she jumped up off the floor, waving a stack of plastic cards in her hand.

"I think I've found what we're looking for. Turn that thing on!"

The microfiche machine took several minutes to warm up. I waited nervously by Brooke's side as she strained to see what was written on the sheets by holding them up to the humming fluorescent lights above our heads. Finally, the light on the machine clicked on and she slid the card under the projection sleeve. Images of birth certificates filled the screen. She began scrolling through, carefully reading each name and birthdate aloud.

"Here's Bill Perkins. And Derek Barnes. I bet we know a bunch more of these kids too. We can rule them out at least." She grabbed her tablet from her backpack and handed it to me. "Here. Type in all the names we don't know as I read them aloud."

She began calling out names of all the baby boys born in the area in the weeks surrounding my supposed birthday. We ended up knowing quite a few of them since we attended different schools growing up. However, by the time we were finished, there were still 27 names on the list.

"That's a lot of names," I said. "How are we going to determine which one might be me?"

"Well, let's think about what we know," she said, scrolling through the names I typed on the tablet. "We know the boy who belongs to the right birth certificate will be missing, because he'll have been you all along. So we're actually looking for missing boys. Boys that have disappeared. There are two 'John Does' in here, so we know they are possibilities."

"How are we going to figure out about the other 25?"

She rubbed the back of her neck and yawned. "I guess we could just search the internet for evidence that these boys have an online presence to confirm they are who they're supposed to be."

"That's not a bad idea. What about the ones that we can't find anything for?"

"I don't know. Let's cross that bridge when we get there. Maybe it'll be just the two John Does left and we can figure out how to deal with them later." She looked at her watch. "I've got to get to the vet clinic. Dr. Hardin is letting me assist on two dog neuters today."

I stood up and helped her return the files to their proper cabinets. "Neuters, huh? I don't know how I feel about you emasculating those poor puppies. Should I be at all nervous that you're learning how to do stuff like that?"

"Maybe you should," she quipped. "It's a pretty useful skill. I've heard it helps keep wayward boyfriends in check."

"I'll keep that in mind should I ever feel compelled to stray." I smiled at her. "Ready to go?"

"Yeah." She turned off the lights, shut the door, and I followed her up the stairs. "On the way back to my house, I'll split up this list and email you half. Then we can each search for some of the names. I should have time to work on mine tonight after work. How late are you working at the club?"

"I'm there 'til close. Then I have to clean up. I won't have time tonight. I was thinking though, now that my father's gone... not my father, I mean, but who I thought was my father." I groaned. "I mean, you know what I mean. Now that he's not around to decide where I should work during the summer, I might quit the job at the country club and go see about that internship at the nonprofit."

"I think that's a great idea. You've always hated working at the club. Plus, it would free up some evenings so I could see you more often."

"That it would," I grinned mischievously as we climbed into my car, "which is always a bonus."

We drove in silence back to her house as she divided the list. The morning had gone better than I expected, and I felt hope, where hours before there was only despair. As always, the effect she had on me was amazing. Without realizing, I began to hum along with the radio.

She looked at me skeptically as we pulled into her driveway.

"What?" I asked.

She looked at me doubtfully. "Do you think you're ready for this?"

"Ready for what?"

"Ready to open this can of worms? Once you do it, you can't undo it, you know? When you start finding out the truth, you'll never be able to 'unknow' it ever again. You'll have to live with the consequences of whatever we find. I'm just saying, you don't have to do this. You can just go on with your life as it is now and accept that you have a mom and sister who love you and leave it at that." She paused, looking at me with concern. "What we find may change your life forever."

"I think you're being a little melodramatic, Brooke. I just want to find out what's happened to my mother. Maybe we'll find her and

34

maybe we won't. And if we do, maybe she'll see me and maybe she won't."

"Either way could be heartbreaking."

I considered her in the passenger's seat. She was truly concerned for my well-being, but I couldn't imagine a scenario I wouldn't be able to handle.

"You said you were on board. That you were sticking with me, right?"

"Yes."

"Then let's soldier on. Can I come over for supper when you get home from church tomorrow?"

"Of course. You know you're always welcome."

"Okay. I'll have my list done by then, and we can regroup and figure out what to do next."

Her shoulders slumped as she turned from me to open the door. I took her arm gently as she slid out of the car.

"I love you, Brooke. Thanks for helping me."

"I love you, too." She leaned back into the car and reached across the center console to kiss me lightly on the lips. "I just don't want to see you get hurt, that's all. See you tomorrow?"

"Can't wait," I said.

CHAPTER FIVE

After a late night managing the wait staff at the country club, I set my alarm to get an early start the next morning tracking down the boys on my half of the list. Of the thirteen names, I was able to find information about all but one of them. Most were easy to locate from high school graduation postings or social networking sites. However, there was no online record of Corbin Brown, born to Patricia and Doug Brown in a hospital across the county just six days before I was born. As much as I was disappointed to have found another lead to explore, I was also excited by the prospect of Patricia and Doug Brown being my birth parents. I couldn't help imagining that perhaps I was the missing Corbin.

I found Mom and Melody eating brunch together at the kitchen table when I finally made my way downstairs just before noon. I spent a great deal of time at work the night before thinking about how indebted I was to them both. I knew they were grieving the loss of my father in their own ways, and that I couldn't allow my anger at him to overshadow my love for them. Brooke's mother's words kept replaying in my head, and I knew if I was going to continue the search for my mother, it would have to be done discreetly and in a way that would be sensitive to my mom's feelings.

Seeing them sitting beside one another as I entered the room, the smell of maple syrup and bacon heavy in the air, made me believe if I tried hard enough, I could convince myself nothing had changed. I squinted hard, trying to pretend my father hadn't died and I hadn't discovered the truth about my adoption. But the truth was there and it wouldn't be ignored.

I watched them for several moments; my mom, mindlessly munching on a slice of bacon, looking through store circulars and Melody, finishing a glass of orange juice while she checked her email on her tablet. They didn't know I was lurking in the doorway spying on them, and I realized in that moment just how grateful I was to have them in my life. I coughed once to alert them to my presence, and they both looked up at me expectantly as I walked across the room.

Mom was cautious, almost wary of me as I poured myself a glass of orange juice from the carton on the table.

"Did you sleep well?" she asked, as she always did.

"I slept some," I replied. "How about you, kiddo?" I said to Melody. "How're you feeling?"

"Tired," she responded. "And sad. And pissed."

"Melody Johnson!" my mom squawked. "You know we don't use language like that in this house!"

I looked at Melody and gave her a wink. "I'm pissed too," I said.

"Charlie!"

"Mom! We're pissed, okay? We're just pissed. And I think if you're honest with yourself, you'll admit that you're pissed too." I paused to look at her, but she was concentrating on the Bigmart ad on the table, unwilling to meet my gaze. "Mom?"

She looked up at me, her eyes glassy and bloodshot. "Yes," she said with resignation. "I'm pissed too."

"Well. There you go," I said. "We're all pissed and there's no one here to take it out on. So what should we do?"

Melody looked suspiciously at me. "So you're not abandoning us?"

"Abandoning you? What do you mean? Why would I do that?"

"Because the other night, you were so mad about not really being my brother. And then you were gone in the morning when I got up. And I never heard you come home last night. And I guess I just thought you were done with us."

The consequences of my impulsive actions on Friday night

smacked me in the face. I was devastated that my little sister, who I loved unconditionally since the day she was born, thought I would forsake her as my sibling. Not only did she lose her father, but she thought she lost her brother as well. My stomach doubled over.

I kneeled before her on the floor and took her hands in mine.

"Melody, I remember the day you came home from the hospital. You were tiny. And all smooshed up. And I thought having a little sister was going to be a giant pain in the butt, especially since I was already eight and knew everything." I could see her sadness beginning to lift, so I continued. "But you were such an amazing little kid, I found myself wanting to be around you. I wanted to play your stupid pony games and princess games and fairy games because you always let me be the hero. And you know what? I'm still gonna be your hero, Mel. I promise. I'm always gonna be your brother and you're always gonna be my sister, okay?"

She looked up at me and wrapped her arms around my neck, squeezing me tightly.

"Okay?" I asked again.

"Okay," she said.

"And we can be pissed about this whole thing together?"

She looked across the table. "You're gonna be pissed along with us Mom, right?

Mom smiled, tears streaming down her face. "Yes, I'll be pissed along with you!" she laughed.

Melody plodded out of the kitchen with a hefty novel under her arm into some hidden corner of the house, and I was left alone with Mom to help clear the table from brunch.

"You're a good brother," she said. "You always have been."

"Not such a great son though," I replied.

She bowed her head. "I'm not angry with you, Charlie. Not even disappointed. I knew this day would come, I just didn't know I'd be facing it alone."

"You're not alone, Mom. I'm here. I'm not going anywhere.

You'll always be my mom, regardless of who else I find out there."

Slowly, she set the plate she was holding into the sink and turned to face me. "What do you mean?" she asked.

I took a deep breath and met her gaze. "I mean that I have to go find her. My birth mother. I need to know who she is. Where she is. Where I come from."

She laid down her dish towel and sat at the table, allowing my words to sink in slowly.

"I'm not leaving you, Mom. I promise."

"I know you say that, and I believe you. I just don't want you to get your heart broken. And someday, I want you to appreciate what your father did for you. He loved you in his way. I know you don't believe it, but he did."

I ignored her comments about my father. I wasn't ready to talk to her about him just yet. "So then you're okay with me searching for her?"

"Could I stop you if I wasn't?"

I considered her for a moment. "No. Probably not."

"Then I might as well support you, but I don't know how to help you. I don't know her name. I don't know where you came from. I don't have any information about her to help you get started. I wasn't a part of any of those conversations. Your father shut me out to keep me from the 'stress of the adoption.' I just signed on the lines where I was told. I do know the adoption was closed. The records will be impossible to get into. It's going to be an uphill battle for you, Charlie." She shook her head and took a deep breath. "I always thought he would be here to give you the information you'd ask for, but now he's not."

"I've got a plan, Mom. Brooke's helping me. We'll figure out who she is one way or another. I'm going over to Brooke's now, for a while, if it's okay with you."

"It's fine." She stood up and slid her arms around my waist. "I love you, Charlie. Just remember while you're searching, there was a reason why she wasn't allowed to continue being your mother. And there's a reason why I was."

Chapter Six

After her father let me in, I found Brooke hunkered down at her family's dining room table behind her laptop and her tablet. She barely raised her head as I sat down beside her.

"Hey, Beautiful," I said, nudging her chin in my direction so I could look at her properly.

"Hey," she replied, finally giving me a smile.

"I figured you would've finished last night. Why are you still searching?" I asked as I scanned her computer screen.

"I'm still searching for three of them."

"Three? That's a lot of missing kids," I said. "Did you try school websites?"

"Yes."

"Social media?"

"Of course."

"Public records?"

"As many as I could find."

"And nothing?"

"Nada."

"Hmm." I stood up and began pacing the room. "So what's that leave us with? The two John Does, your three and the one I couldn't find. So six altogether?"

"I guess so."

"How are we going to find out who or where these kids are?"

Brooke closed her laptop and put it on the floor with her tablet.

She began pulling out placemats to set the table for supper. I took the silverware from the drawer and laid out four place settings.

"It doesn't matter about the kids, Charlie," she said at last. "You're the only kid we care about, right? Searching for them was just a means of narrowing down the list. Now that we have, we're really only interested in the mothers. I think we should just concentrate on finding them."

"You think we'll be able to?" I asked.

"Maybe."

I thought about the possibility of walking up to my mother's house and knocking on the door.

"Do you think if we find her she'll admit the truth to us?"

Brooke stopped what she was doing and shrugged. "I don't know, Charlie. There's only one way to find out."

After cleaning up from dinner with her family, Brooke and I excused ourselves to her bedroom where we continued searching for my mother under her careful supervision. I smiled to myself as I watched her sitting in the middle of her bed, poring over page after page of online phone directory listings and people searches. She always took charge in our relationship. She initiated and planned the trips we took and activities we enjoyed. She was a natural born leader, and most of the time, I just went along for the ride. I didn't mind though. Any path she was on was a path worth traveling, as far as I was concerned.

I remembered our first winter together when she decided out of nowhere she wanted to go skiing. It had been an unseasonably mild winter and there was only a thin base of snow at the local resorts. The closest mountain with heavy accumulation was several hours away and very expensive by college student standards. Although I could have easily afforded to take us for the day, she was determined to get us both there for a reasonable price. After making several phone calls, she secured 25 tickets at a 50% discount, assuming she could sell the lot. After only a week, she started a "Ski Club" on campus and registered enough people to procure the discount. Thanks to her ingenuity, we were able to afford a wonderful weekend together on the slopes, even making some new friends in the process.

The steadfast determination she often displayed was not only admirable, but also reassuring, especially when it came to knowing the search for my mother was in very capable hands.

"Here's the first one," she said excitedly, tossing me her tablet. "Take this down. Sandra Jackson, 38 years old. Her last known address was 5289 3rd Avenue in Burkettsville, across the river. Her son on the birth certificate was named Duane. Couldn't find a trace of him online. Just the same birth record."

"Okay. That's great!" I said. "Burkettsville isn't far. Shouldn't be too hard to call her up and ask about Duane."

She raised an eyebrow in my direction. "You're just gonna call?"

"Why? You don't think so?"

She shrugged her shoulders. "Sure. You can call."

I smiled at her. "You wouldn't call. What would you do? Show up there?"

She grinned at me like a child with a secret. "I'd totally show up there."

"Seriously?"

"Yeah. I'd want to see her. She could lie to you over the phone, Charlie. But we know what your mother looks like. We saw your dad's picture of her. We'll know as soon as we see her if she's your mom."

She had a point, and yet, I was hesitant to barge in on people's lives.

"You really think we should just show up on her doorstep like that? What if she gets angry? Or we upset her?"

"Then we apologize and move on. We only need to see her. We're not moving in."

She was right. God, I loved that girl.

"You're good at this, Sherlock," I said, leaping across the room to tackle her where she sat. I pinned her beneath me and began poking her most ticklish spots.

She squirmed and kicked in an effort to escape. "Watson!" she squealed. "This is not helping to find your mother!"

I kissed her passionately, allowing my body to fit against hers in all the right places. And then I sat up to grin at her. "Alright, then. Let's continue to find my mother."

"You are a bad, bad man, Charlie Johnson," she cried, throwing her pillow at my head. "You can't expect me to concentrate on this when you're offering me *that*!"

"Forget it. I'm not offering anything. Just help me find my mother, woman," I teased.

"I'm not falling for your tricks," she said, repositioning herself on the bed with her computer on her lap. "I'm on to you. Let's just be serious for a little while longer and we'll get this sorted out in no time. Then maybe, if you're lucky, you can thank me."

She always gave as good as she got. In less than ten minutes, she had another name and address for me to write down.

"I've got Beverly Moore. She used to live about 25 minutes away, but now she lives in Petersburg."

"Petersburg? That's a haul."

"Yeah. Tax records show her last known address as 401 South Sycamore Street. Her son's name is Kevin. There's no trace of him anywhere."

"Okay. So two down, four to go," I said.

"Yeah, including the John Does. I say we investigate the ones we have names for and only explore the John Does as a last resort."

I sighed. "Whatever you say, Sherlock."

She peered over her laptop at me. "You know, some would say Watson's role is just as important as Sherlock's. They're a team. Sherlock wouldn't be able to solve the cases without Watson's companionship."

She was attempting to make me feel better about being relegated to the sidelines, but I wasn't going to let her off that easily. I pretended to glare at her.

"That's what I'm good for then? Companionship? Like a dog?"

I could tell from the expression on her face she wasn't sure if I was joking. I couldn't let her suffer any longer.

"Woof woof!" I barked.

"Nice," she said, rolling her eyes as she began scanning the computer screen once again. Minutes later, she tracked down another possibility. "Okay, this one was almost too easy. Patricia Brown gave birth to a son Corbin two days after your birthday at the same hospital. She's still living in the same place on Chester Avenue. The house number is 1135." She glanced up at me. "I'm surprised we don't know this kid. He should have gone to my elementary school but I don't ever remember a Corbin Brown, do you? Maybe he went to private school."

"No," I said, typing in the information. "There was no Corbin Brown in my grade. I don't remember one in the grades around me either. That's strange. Maybe I'm Corbin Brown."

"Maybe," Brooke began, "but don't you think we would have run into Patricia Brown over the years? If she looks like the woman in the picture, I think you might have noticed her."

"I'm pretty oblivious, Brooke."

"That's true," she laughed. "Remember the time I cut bangs in my hair, and it took you three days to figure out what was different about me?"

I rolled my eyes. "Yes. But in my defense, it was in the middle of final exams. My brain was fried. And as I recall, it was the same week you bought those new red shorts. They were distracting to say the least," I said, remembering how cute her butt looked in them.

"Are you kidding me? We're doing the serious work of finding your mother, and you're talking about my butt. Again."

"Your butt is a serious topic."

"You're impossible," she said, returning to her work.

Half an hour later, I was engrossed in a heated game of Football Blitzers on her tablet when she squealed, startling me out of my chair.

"Gotcha!" she cried.

"Who'd you find?

"This last one wasn't easy, but I think I've tracked her down. So," she began, "one Victoria Weddington gave birth to an Andrew Weddington two weeks before your birthdate, three counties over. Just like the others, there was nothing online about Andrew, but unlike the others, there was nothing about the mother either. Victoria Weddington is like a ghost. I wouldn't have known she existed at all except for her son's birth certificate. And then, I just stumbled upon her."

"So where is she?"

"Blakefield Cemetery."

"What?"

"Yeah. She died. I found her death certificate from about nine months ago. And that's not even the most interesting thing about her." She looked up at me dramatically. "Guess who her parents were?"

"Haven't a clue."

"Theodore and Linda Weddington."

I shrugged my shoulders. "I'm supposed to know these people because…"

"Oh my gosh. Seriously, Charlie? Even I recognize the name 'Theo Weddington.'"

I thought for a moment. The name sounded vaguely familiar. Then suddenly, I remembered who he was. "The US congressman?"

"Ding ding. Ladies and gentlemen, we have a winner."

I curled up beside her on the bed as I tried to digest what she discovered. "So let me get this straight. United States congressman Theo Weddington's daughter had a baby boy two weeks before I was born. He's nowhere to be found, and she died about a year ago. Is that it?"

"Pretty much."

"What'd she look like?"

"Victoria?"

"Yeah. Are there any pictures of her online?" I asked, peeking over her shoulder as she scrolled through dozens of images.

"No. It's weird. Like I said before, there's no information about her. As the daughter of a congressman, you'd think I would've found something from whatever prestigious boarding school or Ivy League college she attended. But there's nothing. It's a little strange." She paused. "Or maybe it isn't. Maybe her parents successfully shielded her from the media. Or maybe *she* worked hard to stay out of the public eye. Maybe she didn't want to be anything like her father." She looked at me. "You know something about that."

"That I do," I said, reflecting on Victoria's life.

"If it wasn't for the death certificate, which is of course public record, I wouldn't have found anything about her at all."

"Ok," I said, taking a deep breath, "so we've got four mothers, one of whom is dead, and four missing boys. What's your schedule like this week? Should we plan a road trip to visit the three living mothers to see if I belong to any of them?"

She took her tablet from my hand and scrolled through her agenda.

"I'm off Tuesday. That's it until next weekend. What about you?"

"It doesn't matter. I'll switch with Mullins or just take off. Let's plan on Tuesday afternoon then. Hopefully we can catch them at home after work." I smacked her on the butt. "You in?"

"Are you driving?"

"I'm not letting you drive! The trip to Petersburg would take us until next week!"

"Very funny," she said, punching me in the arm. "We might not even need to go to Petersburg if we find her here, closer to home."

"True," I replied. "But you're still not driving. However, if you're nice, I might treat you to a nice dinner, my lady."

"How chivalrous."

"Am I not always a gentleman?"

"Not always," she grinned, giving me a quick kiss on the lips. "How much longer can you stay tonight?"

I glanced at my watch. It was after seven, and I wanted to spend time with Mom and Melody to show them I was still committed to our family.

"I should go," I said. "Melody is struggling. I need to help her through this."

Brooke wrapped her arms around my waist as I stood up from the bed. "While you're helping everyone else, who's helping you?" she asked.

"You are," I replied. "But I told you before, I don't need help dealing with my father's death. I'm fine. Really. Just help me find my mother so I can put the pieces of my life together and figure out who I am. Then I'll be able to move on."

"Tall order, don't you think?"

"If there's anyone out there that can do it, it's you Brooke Wallace. Of that I have no doubt."

CHAPTER SEVEN

In the wake of my father's passing, the country club's management was more than willing to accommodate my scheduling needs. They happily gave me Tuesday off from my job as the kitchen and wait staff supervisor to spend time with my sister, which was mostly true.

After breakfast, I found her in the back yard, under an enormous elm she spent hours climbing as a child. Her nose was buried in yet another novel, and I made enough noise as I approached to assure I wouldn't startle her.

"Hey, kid," I sat, squatting down beside her on the dew-covered grass.

"Hey, Charlie," she replied.

"Whatcha reading?" I asked.

"Pride and Prejudice."

"I don't think I read that until eleventh grade. And even then it was under duress."

"I like it. I love when Elizabeth and Mr. Darcy finally get together. I feel such relief every time."

"Jeez, how many times have you read it?"

"Eight."

I shook my head. "Okay, well, since you've already read it a few times, what would it take to tear you away from it for a little while today?"

She looked up from the well-worn pages and considered me. "Something with you?"

"Yeah, something with me."

"No Mom, no Brooke?"

"Just us."

Dimples appeared in her cheeks, and I caught a glimmer of excitement cross her face. "Will you take me kayaking on the lake?"

"Sure! And we'll pack a lunch so we can eat at the park picnic tables when we're done."

"Really?"

"Really."

"We haven't done anything fun just the two of us since you were in high school." She paused. "It's been a long time, Charlie."

She was right. Once I went away to college and met Brooke, there'd been less time for her in my life. She accompanied us to the movies and fishing and bowling from time to time, but I hadn't spent any quality time alone with her in quite a while.

"Things are gonna change around here, little sister. I promise," I said, holding out my hand to help her off the ground.

She hesitated to take my hand. "I'm not really your little sister, remember?"

I bent down and picked her up, throwing her over my shoulder. Her book tumbled to the ground, and she squealed and shrieked with delight.

"As long as I can still do this, you will always be my little sister! Got it?"

"Got it!" she squealed.

As we paddled around the lake in the quiet stillness of the morning, our bond as siblings, and more importantly, as friends, was renewed. We talked about the cute boy who treated her to a frozen fudge bar from the pool's concession stand, and about how her best friend's new puppy chewed on everything and pooped on the floor. She confessed that she struggled with fractions and mixed decimals in math, but got tutored by one of her teachers and eventually figured it out. Finally, she confided in me how angry she was at our father for lying to me. And for not making us a priority in his life.

"And for dying," she concluded.

"Me too, Mel," I told her. "Me too."

She stopped paddling and ran her hand through the glass-like surface of the water.

"Do you wish you could use your trip to go back and tell him that?" she asked.

Until the moment she suggested it, I hadn't considered my government sanctioned trip to the past. It suddenly dawned on me that it might be therapeutic to go back in time to tell my father how I really felt. I knew, however, that strict regulations prevented those who traveled into the past from making changes, and so, whatever was done in the past could never be undone.

When time travel was first discovered, there were no laws to sanction its use. In the beginning, scientists worked laboriously to document the problems with traveling, but despite their findings and although they advised against it, the general population eventually began taking trips as well. It was at that point the real dangers became apparent, especially with regard to making changes in the past. As more and more people were traveling back to relive wonderful moments in their lives, some of those infinitesimally small changes began to affect not only the traveler's life, but also the lives of innocent bystanders. Inadvertently, travelers were changing the futures of the people around them without even knowing they were doing it. They would return to the present only to find that people who were once a part of their lives were no longer there. Different career paths were chosen. Loves were lost. Children disappeared. It was a dark period in the history of time travel.

At that point, governments were forced to step in, as generations of people were in danger of having their lives, and more dangerously, other people's lives, irreparably destroyed. Politicians fought bitterly about the crisis. Split evenly on either side of the battle, there were those who believed our ability to time travel was just another evolution of our species that should be allowed to play out accordingly. Others believed the practice should be obliterated and never attempted by humankind again. An agreement was reached by the world's leaders somewhere in the middle.

Beginning with the third generation after the discovery, new laws were put into effect limiting each individual to one trip per lifetime. At birth, all citizens, along with their identification tagging, were coded with one trip voucher. The trip could be used at any point during a lifetime after the age of 18, but was good for just one trip. The duration of the trip could not exceed six months. Classes were required with mandatory attendance three times a week for two months before the trip. In addition, the paperwork was extensive. The decision to time travel was taken quite seriously by most people.

"You know the rules, Mel. Even if I did go back to the time before he died, I couldn't change the past. I didn't tell him what a jerk I thought he was the first time around, so that's it. It's one and done."

"I don't care about the stupid traveling rules. As soon as I'm eighteen, I'm using my trip to make him feel bad for the way he treated you. I'll make him tell you the truth."

"Oh no you won't. If you make him tell me the truth before he dies, everything from that point on will be completely different. That would be way too many years in the past, and you have no idea what type of horrible chain of events you might set off from that point forward. Who knows what could happen." I looked at her seriously. "Promise me you'll never do that."

She stared across the lake without responding.

"Melody? Promise me."

She dragged her hand across the water, splashing me in the face. "I promise," she pouted.

I suggested it might be a good idea to visit the therapist Brooke saw after her brother died. She always spoke fondly of Dr. Richmond, and I suspected she still went to his office from time to time.

"I'll go if you go with me," she relented.

In a moment of weakness, I promised I would.

The conversation was all but forgotten during our delicious lunch of egg salad sandwiches and fresh berries. It wasn't long before we packed up the kayaks and headed home. After dropping Melody off, I was surprised to see it was almost three o'clock by the time I pulled into Brooke's driveway.

She was sitting on the front porch steps, her orange tabby Freckles curled up at her feet. The sun was just beginning to slip behind the tops of the colossal pines surrounding her family's home, and the light and shadows danced across her face. In that moment, I felt as though I'd seen her there before, waiting for me on the porch. It was the most peculiar sense of déjà vu because my memory was not of the exact same scenario, but of one that occurred on a rainy night during high school. And yet, I hadn't met Brooke until college.

"Hey, hot stuff," she said as she strolled toward the car, her backpack flung over her shoulder.

"Hi, yourself," I replied, giving her a kiss as she slid into the passenger's seat. "Did you get a chance to plan out our itinerary?"

"You know I did. First stop is Patricia Brown over on Chester Avenue."

"We've both probably passed that house a thousand times over the years."

"I know. Ready to knock on the door?"

"As ready as I'm gonna be," I said.

Chapter Eight

My confidence waned as I pulled the car up to the curb in front of the house. It was a modest Craftsman-style, tastefully painted and lovingly maintained. There was a practical, midsized car in the driveway. I closed my eyes and imagined returning for holiday meals once Patricia Brown admitted to handing me over to Phil Johnson for reasons she can no longer comprehend. Still, I couldn't bring myself to open the car door.

Brooke immediately sensed my apprehension. "We can head back to your house. Hole up in your bedroom and play video games. No one will ever have to know we researched any of this."

"No. I can do it. I want to do it. Come on." I opened the door and climbed out. Brooke followed me up the sidewalk.

By the time I reached the front door, I was determined to see my plan through. I confidently rang the doorbell and stood back so I could fully see whoever opened the door.

Within seconds, a disheveled looking teenage boy stood before us.

"Yeah?" he said.

"Uh, hi. My name's Charlie Johnson, and this is Brooke, and we are looking to speak with Patricia Brown. Is she home by any chance?"

"Yeah. She's here. She's in her office working. What's this about?"

I looked at Brooke, hoping she would give me a signal as to whether I should discuss the details of our visit with the boy. She shrugged her shoulders, indicating I was on my own.

"We're actually wondering about her son, Corbin."

The boy looked as if I hit him in the gut with a bat.

"What about him?"

I looked at Brooke, and once again, she offered no direction. "I think we should probably just speak to Patricia, if she's available," I said to the boy.

He looked between us, obviously trying to decide if we were legitimate. After several seconds, he stepped aside and allowed us to enter the foyer.

The house was as quaint on the inside as it was from the street. The windows were open, and there was a refreshing cross breeze cooling the space. I heard footsteps coming from the rear of the house. A petite woman in her late 40's entered the foyer.

She was not the woman from the photo in my father's desk drawer. My heart sank, and yet I felt compelled to explain myself for disturbing them.

She smiled. "I thought I heard someone at the door. Can I help you?" she asked politely.

"Hello, Ms. Brown," I began. "I'm Charlie and this is my girlfriend, Brooke. I apologize for disturbing you, but it appears there's been a mistake. I recently found out that I'm adopted, and now I'm looking for my birth mother. I thought you might be her because you had a son, Corbin, around the time I was born. But now that I've seen you, I don't believe you're my mother or that I'm Corbin. I'm so sorry we've wasted any of your time today." I reached for the door to let myself out.

"Wait," she said.

I turned to face her. She appeared to be holding back tears.

"You said you and Corbin were born at the same time?"

"Yes," Brooke chimed in. "Corbin was born two days after Charlie. They were delivered at the same hospital."

Patricia took several steps across the foyer, stopping directly in front of me. Before I understood what she was about to do, she took my face in her hands and gazed curiously at me.

"He would have been your age. A man. I can't begin to imagine him fully grown." She shook her head and removed her hands from my face to wipe away tears from her cheeks. After a moment, she regained her composure and looked at me again. "Do you have a few minutes?"

Brooke responded before I understood what was happening. "Of course, Ms. Brown," she replied.

"Please, call me Patricia," she said. "Come sit down in the kitchen. There's something I want you to see."

Our visit to the Brown residence had taken a surprising turn, and Brooke took my hand as we followed Patricia and her son into the kitchen, where she offered us a seat at the table. After introducing us to Corbin's younger brother Callub, who continued to regard us with a degree of skepticism, she produced a photo album from a bookshelf in the adjacent room, laying it before us on the table. She opened it to the first page.

I could almost hear the newborn baby boy, wearing his tiny knitted cap, wailing at the top of his lungs.

"That's Corbin's first photo," Patricia said smiling. "He screamed for six straight hours after he was born. He was a fighter from day one. I imagine you were probably still at the hospital with us when these pictures were taken, Charlie."

"I suppose so," I replied absently as I carefully turned the next page of the album. Several more baby pictures filled the sheets.

"He's adorable," Brooke commented, smiling at Patricia.

"He was a good baby with the sweetest disposition. He'd just lie in my arms, looking up at me as if there was so much he wanted to tell me if he only had the words." She sighed heavily.

I didn't know what else to do, so I continued to flip through the book.

Each page was filled with picture after picture of Corbin Brown growing up before my eyes. Corbin at a birthday party, riding a pony, splashing in a kiddie pool. Corbin holding his baby brother in his tiny arms. She laughed as she told us the stories which accompanied each of the pictures.

"Look at this one!" she exclaimed, pointing to Corbin wearing a pair of roller skates. "I don't know how he was able to do it, but I remember him flying up and down the sidewalk on those things, the summer he was four. He never ceased to surprise me with the things he could do. He was quite a little boy."

As I turned yet another page, my breath caught in my throat. The spunky child was gone. A sullen one replaced him.

"That one was taken a week before the doctor told us he was sick, just before his fifth birthday. He was tired. All the time. Didn't have the energy of a typical preschooler, you know? He moved into the hospital the day after his diagnosis. He never got to come back home."

I flipped through the remaining pages of the album. Corbin with pale, sunken eyes. A tiny, bald head. Hooked to machines and surrounded by matchbox cars. I couldn't look at the book any longer.

"He'd have been your age. You two would have been in class together, I suppose. Maybe you would have been friends, if he had ever been able to go to kindergarten. It's funny, even with you sitting right here, I have trouble picturing him any older than five. But there you go," she said, picking the album up off the table and cradled it in her arms. "I'm sorry you're not Corbin, and I'm sorry I'm not the mother you're looking for, but it was nice to meet you just the same, Charlie. I hope your story has a happy ending."

I had no idea what to say to Patricia Brown, whose missing son was taken from the world long before his time.

"I'm so sorry for having upset you," I said, rising from the chair, unable to look at her face.

"Is that what you think? That you've upset me? Oh, Charlie, not in the least! It's a pleasure to have met you. Don't think you coming here is what made me sad. I lost a child. Never a day goes by that part of me isn't sad. But it's a great joy to see another child who's grown and making their way in the world. It's comforting to know that life is going on for other children." She was silent as she walked us to the door. "Let me know when you find your mom, huh? I'd like to know how your story ends."

"I'll do that," I said. "It's nice to have met you and Callub. And Corbin, too."

We said our goodbyes, and with that, Brooke and I were back in the car, headed east across town. We didn't speak to one another after leaving the Brown residence, and just before we crossed into the next county, I pulled the car off onto the shoulder. My hands were shaking uncontrollably, and I couldn't steady my breathing.

"I don't know if I can do this," I said, not taking my eyes from the road.

"That was pretty intense," she replied.

"Who would've thought we were going to walk into that? There's no telling what we'll find if we keep searching."

She didn't speak, which was unlike her. I knew she was thinking, considering her words carefully so as not to upset me further.

"What should we do?" I asked finally.

"That depends on how badly you want to meet her."

I wanted to know where I came from. I wanted to know what happened to my mother. Most of all, something Mrs. Brown said struck a chord inside me.

"Do you think it's true what she said, about being sad a little bit every day since Corbin died?"

She looked at me earnestly. "Yes. I miss Branson every day."

"You do?"

"Yeah. I do. Every single day."

"Do you think my mother's out there somewhere missing me?"

She reached out to touch my cheek, gently brushing her fingertips across my stubble. "I don't know," she whispered.

I rested my forehead on the steering wheel and stared at my feet. I didn't want to think about her abandoning me. I didn't want to think about upsetting other families.

"This isn't going to get easier, is it?"

"I don't think so. Corbin Brown's story might just be the tip of the iceberg," she replied.

"Maybe that's why it feels like I'm on the Titanic," I said, pulling the car back onto the highway.

CHAPTER NINE

Our next stop was Sandra Jackson's house, about a 40-minute drive from town. We drove together in silence for most of the trip while I struggled to come to terms with Corbin Brown's tragic death. Then suddenly, I remembered to ask Brooke about Dr. Richmond.

"I spent the morning with Melody."

"Did you have fun?" she asked.

"Yeah. It was good. I need to carve out more time in my life for just the two of us, especially now that our father's gone. She's gonna need some sort of adult male in her life. Isn't that what they say on TV?"

"Charlie, don't kid yourself, you've always been more like a father than a brother to her."

"You think so?"

"Yes! Remember when she was being picked on by the Carroll twins, and you swooped in to defend her? They've never bothered her again."

I cocked my head in her direction.

"What?" she asked.

"I was in high school when that happened. I didn't even know you then. I don't remember telling you about that at all."

A look of trepidation crossed her face. "Oh. That's funny. I guess Melody must have told me about it." She paused. "Now that I think of it, I'm sure that's it. She said she was really glad you stuck up for her, and that it was something your father would have never done."

"She said that? It doesn't sound like her."

"It was something like that. Maybe not word for word." She looked away. "Anyway, it doesn't matter. I was just trying to say it's a wonderful thing that you're spending more time with her because she's gonna need you more than ever, that's all."

I turned back to the road, disquieted by our conversation. It was as if she was hiding something from me, and I didn't like it.

"Anyway," I said, attempting to shake it off, "she's suffering more than I initially thought. She's angry. Probably depressed. What do you think about her talking to your Dr. Richmond? I told her I'd go with her if she wanted me to."

When she didn't respond, I turned again to gauge her expression. The color drained from her face and she appeared frozen in her seat.

"Or, we could choose another therapist to talk to..." I continued.

"No. No. It's fine," she said quietly. "It's actually a wonderful idea. I think she'd really benefit from his help. You would too for that matter."

I knew her well enough to realize something was wrong. The tension between us was growing, and I couldn't put my finger on when I felt the first pang. She and I saw eye to eye on most things. She was always making comments about 'the universe' wanting us to be together, and strangely, I felt the same way. She accepted me, from the minute I met her, just the way I was. No expectations that I would achieve social and financial greatness like the girls I knew in high school. No fear about how the world would view our relationship, or pretenses that it was anything but pure and honest and true.

I reached for her hand across the center console and wove her fingers between my own. "I'm glad you're here," I said.

She smiled and squeezed my hand tightly. "I wouldn't be anywhere else."

The map application on her tablet began to beep, alerting us to our exit and destroying the intimacy of the moment. "You need to get off at the next road and make a left. We're almost there."

Within five minutes we were pulling up the Jacksons' gravel

driveway. The house at the end was a modest double wide trailer with a border of hydrangeas surrounding the front deck.

"You sure this is it?" I asked as I turned off the engine.

"Positive." She grabbed her bag from the back seat and turned to face me. "Whatever we find here, it's all going to be okay."

"I know. I've got you. Let's do this."

We crossed in front of the house and were joined by a large mutt who was clearly more greeter than watchdog, as he almost knocked Brooke over, paws on her shoulders, covering her face with slobbery kisses.

"Rusty! Rusty, get down boy!" called a woman from around the side of the house. Both Brooke and I turned to see who was approaching, and the dog joyfully bounded off in her direction.

A lanky, beanpole of a woman wearing cutoff overalls and a welcoming smile joined us in the front of the house.

"My apologies for the dog. Got kicked out of obedience school for being a bad influence on the others. Twice. I hope he didn't hurt you," she said to Brooke with an accent so thick, I felt sure she was raised in Alabama.

"No, not at all," she replied.

"What can I do for you two this fine day?"

"Well, I'm Charlie and this is Brooke. We're looking for a Sandra Jackson," I told her.

"You're in luck!" she cried. "You found her!"

Brooke and I shared a knowing glance, filled with all the disappointment and relief that came with the woman's declaration.

"Well," I began, "as it turns out, you aren't who we're looking for after all."

"But wait. I just told you I was Sandra Jackson. And that's who you're looking for. So how can I not be who you were looking for when I just told you that I was?"

I couldn't help but smile at the truth of her statement. I tried again to explain the situation.

"You see, I found out recently that I am adopted and I'm looking for my birth mother. I have a picture of her, and now that I've seen you, I know you aren't the woman in the photo and therefore, cannot be the person that I'm searching for."

"Oh," she said, scratching Rusty behind the ears. "What in the world made you think I could've been your momma in the first place?"

"We found a birth certificate for a son you gave birth to around the time I was born. There's no other record of him, and we thought maybe it was because you gave him up for adoption."

Sandra stopped petting the dog and looked at me seriously, as if she was in a trance.

"How old are you?" she asked. "Just turned 21?"

"Yes, Ma'am," I replied.

"My Duane would have been 21 this past April."

"Yes, Ma'am. Me too."

She shook her head and began walking to the door on the side of the house. "There's a reason why you didn't find anything on my Duane," she called over her shoulder. "Come inside for some tea and I'll tell you about him."

I was beginning to wonder why I didn't listen to my own instincts and make phone calls instead of house calls. Clearly, butting into people's lives had consequences. But having a glass of iced tea with Duane Jackson's mother seemed like the least I could do, given the strangeness of the situation. I followed Brooke and Rusty into the house and the screen door slammed behind me.

"Woo, it's been a warm one out there today," Sandra said, pulling the pitcher of tea from the refrigerator. You two want lemon?"

"Sure. Thanks," I replied.

She poured three tall glasses of tea in mismatched tumblers and placed them on the counter.

"Come have a seat on the sofa and bring your tea. Got a couple minutes until Billy gets home from work before I gotta get ready to take off myself. I work third shift over at the factory."

Brooke smiled at me as we followed Sandra out of the kitchen. I knew what she was thinking; that Sandra Jackson was a lonely woman and the least we could do was spare a few minutes of our day. I rolled my eyes and she stuck her tongue out at me. The tension between us dissolved.

"So, you're looking for your birth momma, huh? Funny times we live in. Can't you just go to the adoption agency and have them look it up for you?"

"No, Ma'am. My situation is a bit more complicated than that. I'm having to do my own investigation, and to be honest, it's not going too well."

"I see. I'm mighty sorry to hear that. And I'm sorry you drove out here only to find another dead end. But I can promise you I never gave my boy Duane up for adoption. Might have threatened to at times, mind you, but that kid was the light of my life. I guess you didn't find anything on him because he died when he was 14 in an ATV accident. Happened right around the corner, on the farm down the road." She took a long swig of her tea and set her glass aside. "Not a day goes by I don't think of that boy. He was a good kid. Didn't get in much trouble. Did okay in school. Wanted to be a mechanic like his daddy." She scratched Rusty under his collar and he shook his tail approvingly. "But that's enough about me. Tell me about your momma. Why's it so important that you find her?"

With no compunction, Sandra cut right to the chase. Although I knew she was asking out of sheer curiosity, I was briefly taken aback by her intrusive question. The truth was I hadn't actually stopped to analyze why I felt compelled to find her. There no logical explanation. I had a mom who loved and supported me, and by her account, my birth mother had been deemed unfit to raise me. It stood to reason, if I found her, that she might not be the type of woman who would add anything meaningful to my life. And yet, I still needed to know who she was.

"Do you know when you're watching a really good TV show and it's 9:58 and you know the storyline is never gonna get wrapped up by the credits so you're gonna have to wait until the next week to find out what happens? And you don't know if the story is gonna take a good turn or a bad turn, but it doesn't matter… you just *have* to find out how it ends?"

"Yup. Happens all the time."

"That's what I feel like right now. It's as if I know there's another episode of the show and it might not be a happy ending, but it doesn't matter because it's *my* story that's waiting to be continued. And on the slim chance that my mother might be glad to see me if I find her, I owe it to both of us to look, because maybe she still thinks of me and wants to hear my story too."

Sandra nodded thoughtfully. "I think you may be right about that. You know anything about her?"

I shook my head. "Only that she was forced to give me up because she couldn't take care of me."

"That must have been hard for her."

I considered how she may have felt, and my heart ached, reflecting upon what it must have been like for her when I was taken away. "I guess so," I replied.

Our conversation was interrupted by the sound of car tires crunching across the gravel drive, and Sandra lifted her head to peer out the window.

"That'd be Billy," she said. "Time for me to get ready for work."

"We should probably head out then," I said, standing up from the sofa with my empty glass.

Before I realized what she was doing, Brooke crossed the room and gathered Sandra into her arms. Not surprisingly, Sandra returned her embrace. I couldn't help but smile at how quickly Brooke connected with other people. She never met a stranger.

"It was nice to meet you, and we're both very sorry for the loss of your son," she said. "We hope you have a nice evening."

"You too," she replied, opening the screen door so we could pass through. As I reached the first step, she grabbed my arm. "You know, if I gave a baby up for adoption, I think I'd be happy he wanted to find me. Keep looking. I'm sure she's out there somewhere."

I looked into her eyes. They were warm. And sincere. "Thanks,"

I said, and I meant it.

Chapter Ten

Back on the interstate, Brooke's nose was buried in the GPS once again.

"Just stay on this road until we get closer to Petersburg. It's gonna be a while. Thirty miles or so." She laid her head back on the headrest and sighed deeply.

"Penny for your thoughts?" I asked.

"Not worth that much. I was just thinking I'm an idiot. I should have looked for death certificates for the kids we couldn't find. That would have saved us from bothering those poor women."

"They didn't seem too bothered. In fact, it seemed like they both kind of welcomed the fact someone was interested in their kids."

"I guess." She hesitated. "Do you want me to see if there's a death certificate for the next one? Might save us the drive all the way to Petersburg."

I almost told her yes. But as I considered how I truly felt, I was overcome by a wave of disappointment. Not because of the failure our trip had become, but because I didn't like the thought of ending my adventure with her so soon. I looked away from the road and reached out to turn her face in my direction. "You could. But I *was* looking forward to the drive. Just me and you. And I promised you a nice dinner for your trouble, remember?"

"I do remember," she said smiling. "Where are you thinking?"

"I was thinking the café with that great barbeque, where we stopped on the way home from the beach last year."

"That *was* good," she replied. She set down her tablet. "Okay, you've convinced me. We're already on the way. Let's just stay the course."

"Alright," I declared, pounding the steering wheel with both hands. "Brooke and Charlie, staying the course. That's what I like to hear!"

"You're a nut, you know that?" she laughed.

"I'm nuts about you," I replied.

She was suddenly serious, once again. Her face fell, her smile fading. She turned from me to look out the window, but I knew she wasn't concentrating on the miles of farmland passing by.

It never bothered me that she was a serious person. In fact, I thought she was a refreshing change from many of the shallow, frivolous women I met throughout my life. Brooke was an old soul, in many ways. She was quiet and reflective, and it took a bit of instigation to encourage her outgoing side into the light. Her brother's death affected her in ways I would never understand. I imagined when he died, he took a bit of her spirit with him. I would have relished the opportunity to have spent just one day with her before that tragedy, if only to see what she was like while her spirit was still whole.

I learned over the years when it was best to leave her alone, and also, the times when she could be persuaded to bare her soul. Since my father's death, she'd become more reserved than usual, and I saw the car's confinement as an opportunity to lure her out of her proverbial shell.

"Two down, two to go," I said cheerfully.

She scoffed, shaking her head. "It amazes me that you can be so..."

"So what?"

"So completely glib about this whole thing. Your father dies. That's bad enough. But then on top of that, because I'm a big 'Snooper McSnooperson,' you find out he's not really your father. And oh, by the way, your mom's not really your mom and your sister's not really your sister. And so now, here we are, barging into people's lives, searching for a mother who was deemed unfit to parent, for whatever reason, like we're on spring break."

"Brooke, I don't…"

"Wait. I'm not done. The worst part is that you have yet to deal with the emotional ramifications of losing your father. What you're doing instead is redirecting the energy you should be spending on that going on this wild goose chase search for your birth mother. It's just a way for you to bury the pain so you don't have to deal with it."

"Do you really…"

"I was not finished! And if all of that wasn't concerning enough, I just know down deep, whoever we find or don't find out there is not going to be who you want her to be, and then you're going to have yet *another* disappointment to bury and ignore. And I, for one, can't watch you do it."

I remained silent, fearful of interrupting her again. I had no idea I was sitting beside a dormant volcano on the verge of eruption. And now I felt as though I was covered in molten lava. I waited patiently for her to cool down. Finally she spoke.

"I'm finished now," she said placidly.

I laughed. I couldn't help it. She never stayed angry for long.

"You sure?" I asked.

She gave me a sideways glance and tried desperately not to smile. I knew she was attempting to hold her ground. "I'm serious, Charlie. You have some major issues to deal with."

"Duly noted."

"You need to go talk to Dr. Richmond. Or someone."

"Fine."

"You need to figure things out."

"That's what I'm trying to do."

She groaned. "You're exasperating, you know that?"

"So I've been told."

She went back to staring out the window for several minutes before turning to face me, placing her hand on my knee, just beneath the hem of my shorts. The sensation of her touch gave me goose bumps.

"I thought that I could, but now I don't know if I can do this," she said.

"Do what?"

"Be an accomplice on a mission that has such a high probability of ending in sadness."

"Why's it gonna end in sadness?"

"Because, Charlie, there's a lot more sadness in life than happy endings. I know that better than anyone."

For a split second, my heart stopped beating in my chest. I suddenly realized what triggered her outburst. As much as she was concerned for my happiness, she was concerned for herself as well. In her short life, she'd already dealt with the horrific pain of losing her brother, and until that moment, I hadn't considered the affect my father's death was having on her. Now, in the search for my mother, we'd encountered two more deaths and two more grieving mothers in the course of an afternoon. Perhaps being around so much sadness was causing the painful memories of losing Branson to resurface.

Dealing with her brother's death was something she rarely discussed. It was the one part of her life she kept shut deep inside. I respected her privacy but now wondered what else happened during that period to cause so much inner turmoil.

"You're so strong, Brooke. Stronger than you give yourself credit for. And we have each other. We always have each other. We can get through anything." I paused, remembering her own words. "Aren't you always saying the universe wants us to be together? Maybe this is the reason why. Maybe you're the one who's supposed to see me through this, because you're the only one strong enough to do it."

She peered up at me. Her eyes were full of apprehension, but within them, I could also see the tiniest glimmer of hope. "You think so?"

"Yes. I know so. In fact, I've never been so sure of anything in my life."

Her GPS started beeping frantically. She directed me to take the next exit off the interstate and then quickly changed the subject.

"So, Beverly Moore could be your mom."

"Sounds like a good name for a mom. Should I change my name to Charlie Moore?"

"No. I like Charlie Johnson better than Charlie Moore. And besides, I've already spent hours practicing signing my name 'Brooke Johnson.' You can't change it on me now."

"You're kidding," I said.

"Hey! You're the one who just confirmed the universe wants us to be together. Might as well get a head start on the monogramming."

"You really are mental," I teased, although I wasn't upset by the thought of Brooke sharing my last name.

The GPS began to beep again. "Turn here," she instructed, ignoring my jab. I made a quick right hand turn, practically throwing Brooke into my lap. "There it is. Just up ahead."

We reached the address listed for Beverly Moore, mother to Kevin Moore, whoever he was. It was a sprawling two story brick home, situated on at least an acre of well-manicured lawn. It was an interesting section of town, a suburban feel inside the city limits. There were no cars in the driveway and no lights on at the house. My heart sank.

"And *this* is why we should have called first," I said, opening the car door.

"We can always just go have dinner and then come back," she offered.

"Let's at least go knock on the door. Maybe her car's parked in the garage."

Sure enough, after ringing the bell several times, there was no answer from inside. I noticed the morning's paper on the front porch, yet another indication no one was home.

"Now what?" I asked, as we headed back toward the street. "We don't even know if this is the right place."

"Let's come back a little later," she replied.

We were just getting back into the car when a mid-sized SUV slowed in front of the house and pulled into the driveway. After several seconds, a sharply dressed African American woman stepped out of the vehicle.

Brooke and I exchanged glances. "I guess she's out," I said quietly.

"You don't know that," she whispered. "Maybe Beverly Moore moved and this is someone else. You should ask, just in case."

The woman looked at us skeptically as she pulled her briefcase from the passenger's side of the truck. "Can I help you?" she asked.

I took a step in her direction. "Are you Beverly Moore?"

"Who wants to know?"

I introduced myself as I walked up the driveway, extending my hand in greeting. She shook my hand firmly, clearly annoyed by our presence, but not irate.

"Well, yes, I'm Beverly Moore. What is this all about?"

After concisely explaining my situation, I apologized for the imposition. She assured us it was no big deal, and quickly headed toward the house without making any further small talk. However, as Brooke and I were climbing back into the car, she called to us from the porch.

"He was killed in a drive-by shooting while he waited for the school bus. Ten years old. Straight A student. Never saw it coming. Police said it was gang related, but no one was ever arrested." She opened the front door of the house and stepped inside without looking back. "That's why you didn't find my son in your search."

She shut the door behind her and turned on the porch light. Brooke and I wasted no time buckling our seatbelts, and we were halfway down the street before I finally stopped holding my breath.

"That was tough," Brooke said.

"Yeah. I feel bad we disturbed her. What a horrible tragedy. She's obviously still really angry about it."

"Wouldn't you be angry if your son was killed in a senseless act of violence and no one was ever held accountable?"

"Yeah. Of course."

My head hurt. I was beginning to think we were searching for my mother in all the wrong ways. "So, three strikes."

"Three strikes, but we're not out yet. We still have to explore the possibility that Victoria Weddington is the one."

With an afternoon of disappointment behind me, I was finding it difficult to stay positive. "I don't know, Brooke. What are the chances she's my mother? Even if she is, she's dead. It's not like I'm going to learn anything from her."

"That's true, but her parents are still alive. They might be able to provide some valuable insight into the details of your adoption. And they might know who your father is."

I stretched my back against the car seat. I didn't want to talk about it anymore. My heart and my head needed a break from questioning who I truly was. I just wanted to hang out with Brooke and forget about how completely lost I felt. I wanted to make her laugh. I wanted to see her smile. I wanted to pretend we were young and in love, and that nothing else mattered.

"I'm proposing a moratorium on any conversation surrounding my father, my mother, or any plans regarding either one of them henceforth. From this point forward, until tomorrow, those who do not follow the rules will be shot on sight. Objections?"

She giggled. "No, Sir."

"Perfect. Then direct me, beautiful navigator, to the café where dinner awaits us!"

We shared a delicious meal of barbequed ribs and for a few hours, it was almost as if time was standing still. It was just the two of us, Brooke and Charlie, without a care in the world. All the while, there was a little voice in the back of my head cautioning me just how fleeting the moment would be.

CHAPTER ELEVEN

I spent several weeks attempting to 'work out some of my issues,' as Brooke suggested. Between family time and double shifts at work, I made time to join Melody at Dr. Richmond's office on a Thursday afternoon. With his laid back approach and empathetic demeanor, it was easy to understand why Brooke was fond of him. After reassuring us it was normal to be feeling angry, hurt, and broken, he suggested valuable techniques to help Melody move through the grieving process in a healthy way. He also suggested we meet alone to discuss my relationship with my father, and although I told him I would try to find time in my schedule, I had no intention of returning. I knew there was only one way to fix what was wrong with me, and talking about Phil Johnson wasn't part of the solution. Figuring out my place in the world would begin and end with my mother.

I spent a great deal of time fixating on Victoria Weddington. I devoted the better part of three days digging around the internet, looking for information about her. But just as Brooke discovered, there was little to be found. I didn't find a single photograph. No newspaper articles. No school records. If it hadn't been for her son Andrew's birth certificate and her own death certificate, I might have believed she never actually existed.

The more I thought about her, the more I couldn't imagine a congressman's daughter being an addict, forced to give her child up for adoption. Certainly her family would have never allowed something like that to have happened. Indiscretions of that sort didn't happen in prestigious, well-known families. Drug-addicted mothers were an impoverished, inner city hardship, not a predicament of the suburban elite.

Despite all the indications that Victoria Weddington was not my mother, I couldn't shake the feeling that she was. I began having nightly dreams about the woman in the photograph. She returned to me as soon as I fell asleep, asking me repeatedly why I didn't want to be her son. With each passing night, the dreams became more vivid and distressing. By the fifth night, I woke to the sound of my own labored breathing and found myself shaking, dripping in sweat. I was suddenly convinced beyond a shadow of a doubt that I was Andrew Weddington. Without thinking, I picked up the phone and called Brooke. She answered groggily on the fourth ring.

"Charlie? What is it?" she slurred.

"Victoria Weddington is my mother."

I could hear her yawning. It took her several seconds before she spoke again. "We just talked about this yesterday. You said you were convinced that she wasn't your mother. What in the world has changed your mind?"

"The very thing that convinced me she wasn't is now convincing me that she is."

"I'm not following. I'm tired, Charlie. What time is it?"

I sat up and looked at the clock on my nightstand. It was three in the morning.

"Oh, God, Brooke, I'm sorry. Go back to sleep. We can talk about this later."

"No. No. It's fine. I'm waking up. You must be pretty convinced to call me out of nowhere in the middle of the night. Now go on. Explain it to me again."

"It's just that, I've been thinking all along that the story my mom told me about my birth mother being unfit to care for me because of drugs didn't fit the image of the wealthy daughter of a US congressman."

"Okay. So what's changed?"

"I just dreamt about her. About her family. And in my dream hers was a lot like mine. Just think about my family, Brooke. We're a mess. Families like ours, we only share the version of ourselves we want the public to see. The glossy 8x10 version, not the awkward candid shot. We don't tell the truth. We don't tell the world that we hate our fathers and we're completely dysfunctional."

There was silence on the other end of the line.

"So if your family hides secrets about the kind of people you really are, why wouldn't the Weddingtons be doing the same thing," she said finally.

"Bingo," I replied.

Brooke sighed heavily into the phone. "So what does all this mean, Charlie?"

"Well, it means there's a good chance the Weddingtons are my grandparents. If that's the case, they might know who I am then, right? They would know about their daughter being pregnant and giving birth, don't you think?"

"I suppose," she said.

"And even if they don't, they might be able to help me find the information I'm looking for just the same."

The wheels in my head were already spinning at a tremendous speed, devising a plan which included a trip to the Weddington estate. I was sure I'd have no trouble finding the answers I was looking for within its walls.

"You work the afternoon shift today?" I asked.

"Yeah." She paused, and I could almost hear her rolling her eyes in loving annoyance. "I already know where this is going, Charlie. I'll go with you, but you don't even know if he's around. He might not even be home. He could be in DC."

I hadn't considered whether congress was in session and was briefly taken aback, but I quickly recovered. "Even if he's not there, she should be. She might have more information than he would anyway. A mother would definitely know about her daughter's pregnancy."

She laughed weakly. "Well, since you have everything figured out, can you at least let me get a few more hours sleep before you whisk me off on the next leg of your pursuit?"

"Yeah, of course. I'm sorry. Go back to sleep and I'll call you in the morning. Well, later in the morning. You know, after the sun's up."

She laughed again. The bright, melodic laugh that instantly made my heart ache with longing. "I love you, Charlie. Call me later. When normal people are up."

"I love you too, Brooke."

As I hung up the phone, it struck me just how lucky I was to have someone in my life who would not only answer a call in the middle of the night, but would welcome the conversation. She was beautiful, she was funny, and she was my best friend. I talked myself out of driving across town in my pajamas to sneak through her bedroom window as I'd done so many times before. During our first summer together, I mastered the art of silently scaling the porch rail beneath her room. I spent many pre-dawn hours tucked beneath her covers, before slipping away as quietly as I'd come before sunrise. But on this occasion, I knew she needed to sleep. And frankly, so did I.

I stared at the ceiling, making a mental list of everything I wanted to research in the morning. But after only a few minutes, I gave in to the cacophony of ideas fluttering around my head, like gnats on a summer day, and got out of bed. I threw on my robe and booted up my laptop, which sprung to life, blinding me in the darkness. Without hesitating, I typed 'United States Congressional session dates' into the search engine. I was excited to find they were on break, which meant there was a good chance Weddington would not be in DC. It dawned on me that they could be on vacation, but I quickly thrust that possibility out of my mind. They needed to be home. There was no other option.

Next, I began the search for the location of his residence. I knew he was living in Virginia; I just didn't know how far away he might be. I found traditional search techniques were not providing the information I was looking for, and that discovering his address was going to take far more detective work than I was expecting. At long last, I backed into the information through a channel of public tax records. Seeing the address flash onto the screen brought an immediate sense of fulfillment and relief. It took almost an hour, but I finally did it. I was giddy to discover his estate was less than an hour's drive away, and even though I was only grinning on the outside, I was doing a touchdown end zone dance worthy of a penalty on the inside.

I watched out the window as the silhouettes of the trees began turning from grey to soft rose. I stretched and stood from my computer, considering what to say when I confronted the people I now believed to be my grandparents. I came to realize their daughter may have hidden the pregnancy from them, as it was the only explanation I could rationalize for why they hadn't been willing to take me in as their next of kin. I decided to assume they didn't know I existed and wing it from there. Plus, I had Brooke. She was blessed with the uncanny ability to react normally in the most bizarre of situations.

I waited until just after 7 o'clock before making my way downstairs, fully dressed and ready to start the day. I found Melody eating a bowl of corn flakes at the kitchen table.

"What's up, Squirt?"

She looked up and met my gaze. Dark circles framed her eyes and her complexion seemed sallow. "I heard you up in the middle of the night talking to Brooke. Why are you up so early?" she asked.

"Oh jeez, sorry I woke you…"

"You didn't wake me," she said, taking another bite of cereal. "I haven't really been sleeping."

"You wanna talk about it?"

"No. Not really. My mind's just sort of going all the time. About Dad. And you. And everything else." She stared into her bowl as though the secrets of the universe dwelled within. "You're all dressed up like you have somewhere to go?"

"Am I?"

She shook her head. "Where are you going, Charlie?"

I felt as though I was being interrogated by my own sister, but was reluctant to discuss the search for my mother for fear of upsetting her in any way. "Brooke and I are just going to take a little drive today."

She took another bite of cereal. "Can I come?"

I sat beside her at the table. I didn't want to tell her the truth. It would have been easier to lie. But lying was something that was no longer in my repertoire. "We're going to see some people I think may be my biological grandparents."

She looked at me blankly as if I told her I was going out for eggs and milk. "Okay. So can I come?"

I hadn't planned on the extra company, but I certainly wasn't going to keep her from joining us, as long as she actually wanted to come.

"You're okay with helping me track down my mother?"

"Of course. You're my brother. There's nothing I wouldn't do to help."

She had always been wise and compassionate for her age. I hadn't considered her as an ally in the search for my mother, but here she was, surprising me with her maturity.

I grabbed a banana from the table and slid my tablet into my knapsack. "I'll leave a note for Mom and meet you in the car in five minutes. Can you be ready?"

A glimmer of something passed across her face. Something that almost struck me as excitement. She jumped up from the table and headed for the door before I could react.

"Meet you in the car," she called over her shoulder, with a twinkle in her eye as she bounded up the stairs.

Chapter Twelve

Brooke and Melody spent the entire drive to Weddington's house embroiled in a fascinating discussion about the risqué bathing suits everyone was wearing at the lake and the lack of attractive leading men in the summer's new movies. Just when I thought I was going to have an opportunity to join the conversation, Melody inquired about the best waterproof mascara. It was at that moment I realized my Y chromosome would prevent me from having an opinion about anything they discussed, so I resigned myself to the role of chauffeur and quietly eavesdropped on their schoolgirl banter. Brooke's upbeat nature had an intoxicating effect on Melody's mood, and I was grateful I'd invited her along. Listening to them together, I couldn't help but be enchanted by the warmth of their friendship.

However, once we arrived at the sprawling estate, I became increasingly despondent as my resolution weakened. I pulled around the circular drive, and parked just shy of the marble staircase leading to the front door. A pair of stone lions, ominously resting upon massive stone pillars at the base of the staircase, defied me to continue, and the confidence I felt at three in the morning was no longer strong enough to encourage me out of the car. Brooke and Melody sat silently, waiting for me to open the door, but I remained firmly planted in the driver's seat.

Brooke rested her hand on my thigh.

I could not move. It seemed as if my hands were soldered to the steering wheel.

I expected her to urge me on, but it was Melody's voice that surprised me from the back seat. "It's time to find your truth, Charlie. Go on. See what they have to say about your mother."

Her words compelled me into action, and I turned to look at my sister as I opened the door. The little girl I encouraged through gymnastics tryouts, swim meets, and science fair projects was now supporting me.

"I love you guys. I'll be back," I said, my voice thick with apprehension as I stepped out of the car.

The lions glared at me as I strode past and made my way up the steps. The stately three-story brick colonial was shaded by elm and birch trees from the side garden and the stone foundation indicated the home was probably built prior to the civil war. As massive as it was beautiful, it did nothing to ease my anxiety as I stood before the oak door. I hesitated, not knowing whether to knock or ring the bell. I took a deep breath and pressed the bronze button.

Almost immediately, a crisply dressed gentleman with broad shoulders and a stocky frame opened the door and invited me inside. He was built more like a bodyguard and less like a butler, and I wondered what I was getting myself into. Before I finished explaining the reason for my visit, an elegant looking woman with a tightly pulled salt and pepper chignon entered the foyer. She wore a trim pantsuit and an air of superiority. I recognized her immediately from the congressman's website as his wife, Linda. I searched her features for any resemblance to my own but I saw nothing to indicate we were related in any way.

"May I help you?" she asked in a tone suggesting I'd interrupted something important.

"My name is Charlie Johnson," I began, "and I was wondering if I could have a moment to speak with either you or Mr. Weddington?"

She smiled smugly at me. "*Congressman* Weddington is a very busy man. And I'm expected at a speaking engagement at one. Have you made an appointment with my husband?"

My heart sank. "No, Ma'am."

"Oh. Well, then, have a good day," she said, turning back in the direction from which she came.

Every cell in my body seemed to be vibrating at the same frequency and I knew I couldn't let her walk away. "No, wait!" I cried. "I need to ask you about your daughter, Victoria!"

She froze mid-step and slowly turned to face me. There was something akin to recognition in her gaze.

"What about Victoria?"

I was reluctant to continue because I sensed that she had no intention of assisting me, regardless of what I had to say. And yet, I knew my options were limited.

"I was wondering what you could tell me about the child she gave birth to 21 years ago."

Although she was obviously well-trained in human relations, I was able to catch the panic that flickered briefly across her face before it was quickly masked by a false sense of outrage.

"How dare you!" she bellowed. "Whatever you've heard are lies and false accusations!"

"No, Ma'am. I haven't heard anything," I stammered. "I was just wondering what happened to the baby?"

I heard a second voice from within the house but couldn't make out what was being said.

"It's nothing, dear," she called over her shoulder, "just a kid who is on his way out."

I knew I was about to have the door shut in my face, and when it did, I would lose my only opportunity to discover the truth about Victoria's baby.

"Please, Mrs. Weddington," I begged, "I think I may be her son."

For an instant, her face softened, and my breath caught in my chest, hoping she was about to divulge some piece of information. Something to confirm what I already presumed to be true. She stared at me suspiciously, and my heart thumped heavily as I waited for her to respond.

She took a deep breath, pulling herself to her full height before she spoke. "I have no idea what you are talking about young man, but may I suggest you leave the property immediately before I call the authorities to have you arrested for trespassing."

I became frantic. "But please," I cried, "what happened to her son?"

Her words cut like knives. "There. Was. No. Son. See him out, Francis."

There was a hand on my shoulder. The tapping of heels as she fled from the room. The door slamming in my face.

As I stood on the front porch, shaded from the sun by grand Georgian columns, mimicking those of the Capitol in which Weddington spent most of his days, I shivered. I had failed.

Inside the car, Brooke and Melody greeted me with apprehensive faces. I bowed my head in solemn defeat and neither spoke as I drove away from the house. It was Brooke who finally broke the silence almost 15 minutes later.

"Maybe this is the universe telling you to just let things be. You have a good life, Charlie. Even if you never find out what happened to her, you're still gonna be okay."

She was trying to console me, but her words drove an unintended wedge between us. My carefully suppressed anger began to simmer beneath the surface once again. I was suddenly jealous of her perfect, loving family, and furious at how quickly she dismissed my desire for the truth about my own biological ties. I knew if I spoke, I was going to say something I'd regret, so I continued to drive without taking my eyes from the road.

Brooke and I rarely fought, and when we did, it was usually due to a misunderstanding. She was quick to internalize simple, thoughtless comments, and I had difficulty reading and responding to her ever changing moods. Our first Christmas together, she suggested celebrating with her family early in the day. I made an offhand remark about my family not being nostalgic enough for her Victorian sensibilities. Of course, she became upset, assuming I didn't value her family's traditions, which were particularly important to her since

Branson's death. Sadly, by the time I realized my mistake, the damage was already done. I still regretted having spent Christmas day apart that year, and I knew it was only because I hadn't been more careful with her heart. Remembering this misstep reminded me that her comments about the search for my mother came out of genuine concern, and after several silent minutes, I was able to reply. I attempted to reason with her using the only weapon in my arsenal. Branson.

"If there was a chance, any chance at all that you could have discovered why Branson got sick so you could save him just by digging a little deeper and trying a little harder, would you have done it?" I asked.

She was silent. When she didn't respond immediately in the affirmative as I expected, I turned to see her face. Her rosy complexion was blanched, and she was staring at her hands folded in her lap.

"Brooke?"

She turned to me with tears in her eyes. She bit her lip, returning her gaze to her hands. "I'd be just as pigheaded as you're being," she finally replied.

I couldn't help but grin at her. "Pigheaded, huh?"

"Yes. Pigheaded. But I get it. I really do, Charlie. It's just that…" She trailed off.

"I know. You think I'm going to get hurt. I've got it."

She was worried. I couldn't imagine why, but it was nice to know that she loved me enough to be involved. I could count the people in my life who were genuinely concerned for my well-being on one hand. It was comforting to know she was one of them.

"So now what?" she asked.

"How about lunch?" I sighed, defeated.

"No, silly," she said. "What about finding your mother. It seems like we've hit a brick wall."

"I have an idea," Melody chimed in from the back seat.

I looked at her in the rear view mirror. "Do tell, little sis."

"What if you used your trip to go see Victoria?"

It was the second time she brought up time travel and the second time the mention of it caught me off guard.

It was a funny thing, the presence of time travel in our society. One would think it would take more of a precedence in our day to day lives, but the reality was, I rarely thought about that option in my life. Traveling back in time was something other people did, but I never really had the desire.

My father explained about the existence of time travel to me when I was just five years old. He told me, since I was going to school for the first time, I would probably hear about going back in time from the other children, and he wanted me to know the truth. He explained how dangerous it was, citing different ways people's lives were ruined by going back too frequently, which resulted in the government allowing each of us only one trip. He also said I never needed to worry about using my trip because it would never be necessary. Life, he said, was about moving forward. Not backward. And so, for most of my life, I never even considered using my trip.

But in seventh grade, my science teacher and her husband celebrated their 25th wedding anniversary by going back in time together to relive their honeymoon. I have no idea why she chose to tell us she was going. Trips are practically instantaneous in the present timeline, as travelers leave and return on the same date, regardless of how long they are gone or how far back they choose to travel. Therefore, if she hadn't told us, we would have never known she was gone, but I suppose excitement prevented her from keeping it a secret. She was one of the few people I knew to have used her trip, although I assumed others had but simply chose not to disclose it. After class that day, I overheard her gushing to a fellow teacher about how glorious it was to see Paris with her husband once again. It was the first time I ever considered using my trip.

After that, there was a short period in my life when I let the prospect of time travel consume me. I began reading stories online and in books, trying to understand the reasons why people chose to go back in time. I laid in bed at night imagining what I would choose to relive when I was older. I considered changing the past, even though I knew it was strictly forbidden. I became fascinated by the horrifying accounts of those who made unexpected changes to their timelines which led to catastrophic results. It was the first time in my life I considered using my trip as a way to find out the truth about the secrets my parents were keeping from me.

I blinked twice, as if to bring myself from a daze, and smiled brightly at my sister. "Now that's not a half bad idea!"

"You could go back to before she died and ask her if she's your mother."

"That's a horrible idea," Brooke interjected sternly.

I furrowed my brow at her. "No, it's not. It's a great idea."

"Going back in time is a horrible idea. No good can come of it," she said, crossing her arms atop her chest defiantly.

I couldn't understand why she was having such a visceral reaction to the suggestion of going back in time to see Victoria.

"Brooke, think about it. Going back to see her is really the only way I can find out for sure if she's my mother." I watched her seething in the seat beside me. "I think I'm going to look into it."

She didn't speak. She didn't even move.

"Brooke?" I said, reaching across the center console to place my hand on her knee. As soon as I touched her, she recoiled, pulling her legs to the side, just beyond my reach.

"I won't help you do it," she said finally.

And just like that, I lost her. She retreated into her own thoughts and refused to speak to Melody or I for the remainder of the ride home. I had no idea why the idea of using my trip made her so angry. She clearly had issues with time travel we had never discussed. I was hesitant to upset her further by pressuring her to discuss the reason for her objections, so instead, as we approached the city limits, I offered to take her home.

"I love you," I said as we pulled into her driveway.

"If you love me, you'll forget about using your trip. I'm begging you."

"I can't promise you that," I said. "But I can promise that I'll find a way to get the information I need without changing the past so I can come straight back here to you."

Glaring at me, she leaned her head back into the car through the passenger side window. I'd never seen her so agitated.

"If only it was that easy," she spat at me. "I'll help you find another way to track down your mother, but if going back in time is the path you choose, I won't support you, and I won't be waiting for you when you get back."

She turned on her heel and headed toward her house, slamming the screen door behind her as she disappeared inside.

"I'm so sorry, Charlie," Melody began to cry. "I shouldn't have said anything. Now you and Brooke are fighting and it's all my fault."

"No, it's not. We'll be fine, you'll see," I told her. But as I said the words, I had trouble believing them myself. My best option was to find a way to convince Brooke that going back in time wasn't as terrible as she thought. The only problem was how to do it.

Chapter Thirteen

I decided to give Brooke time to cool down. I didn't call. I didn't text. I hoped that perhaps she would come to see things my way, but sadly, as I sat in front of the television watching mindless sitcoms with my mom, my phone remained silent in my pocket. I hated not speaking to her, and the thought of not having her support tore me up inside.

She was always my cheerleader, regardless of the situation. When my father gave me a hard time about not attending Harvard in front of several hundred people at my uncle's retirement party, she bravely spoke up to defend my decision. After a rash of car vandalism on campus, she happily led a campaign to install street lights on the unlit parking lots. And during the fall of my junior year, when I decided to drop my minor in economics in favor of a dual major in business and sociology, Brooke helped me break the news to my less than enthusiastic father.

There were also times when she didn't agree with my decisions but supported me just the same. Those were the times that meant the most. Like when I chose to skip a swim meet in favor of attending my roommate's cover band performance at a dive bar in the city. She scolded me for bailing on my obligation to the team, but stood beside me in front of the stage, singing along like a maniac.

As I lay in bed, throwing a football into the air above my head, I thought about calling her. And I thought about going back in time. The more I considered Melody's idea, the more I realized how badly I wanted to find out the truth about Victoria. I knew there was no information online about her and, after the frigid reception I received at her parents' house, I knew they would never give me the information I needed. Using my trip to find out the truth seemed like a reasonable and viable solution to the problem. I just didn't understand why Brooke was so opposed to the idea.

By eleven o'clock, I couldn't stop myself from reaching out to her. I sent her a quick text which read, 'I value your opinion. I'd like to talk. I love you.'

After pressing send, I waited. The screen remained blank. I threw myself across the bed and tossed my phone onto the floor. Seconds later, I heard the familiar beep of an incoming text. I scrambled across the carpet and picked up the phone.

'I'll meet you tomorrow. At our spot. 9:00. There's something you need to know. And… I love you too.'

It took everything I had not to call. Or drive to her house so I could stand below her bedroom window to see her. I couldn't imagine what she needed to tell me that I didn't already know. But I knew I needed to be patient. So I slid between the sheets of my bed, closed my eyes, and hoped that my mind would allow sleep to find me quickly.

By 8:45 I was already parked just off the side of the road, along the guard rail at the trailhead entrance that led to the falls. To call it a waterfall was a slight misnomer. It was actually more of a short drop in elevation in a small section of the river. However, the drop was steep enough that the water made an impressive crashing sound as it made its descent. During fall break, only a few weeks after we met, Brooke planned a hiking trip to the falls together as one of our very first dates. She packed a picnic lunch of fried chicken and carrot sticks, and we sat together for hours on a threadbare comforter, sharing the secrets of our lives.

It was the very first time she told me about losing Branson.

She didn't cry when she described the horror of his disease or the pain of watching him endure it. She spoke with quiet resignation in her voice, saying the beauty of his life was that she was able to share it with him, if only for a little while. During that initial conversation, I assumed incorrectly that her lack of fury over the loss of her brother was simply because she hadn't been as close with him as I was with my own sister. It took several months before I came to realize how deeply she had loved him and that her acceptance of his passing was something she fostered over time. Somehow, she moved past the pain and found peace.

It was on that day, in front of the falls, the din of the cascading water muffling our voices, that I told Brooke I loved her for the very first time. It came out of my mouth before I realized what I was saying. Perhaps it was the way the sunlight danced in her hair, reflecting strands of copper and gold as she raced ahead of me through the forest, determined to beat me to the falls. It could have been her willingness to share her pain with me before knowing fully how I would react to the struggle she'd endured. Or maybe it was simply the calm I felt inside myself whenever she was beside me. Whatever the reason, I spoke the words.

And for whatever reason, she spoke them right back.

I watched with great anticipation as she approached from the opposite direction, parking her car nose to nose with mine. She raked her fingers through her hair and piled it on top of her head into a loose ponytail. Finally, after fumbling around inside her car for several moments, she looked up at me and waved, a weary smile on her lips.

I met her on the side of the road and took her hand in mine. Her fingers were chilly and I folded them carefully between my own to warm them.

"Hi," she said finally.

"Hey," I replied. "Did you bring a blanket?"

"No. I don't have a lot of time. I need to be at the clinic by ten o'clock, so I thought we could just hike in. We won't be able to stay."

I was disappointed. "It's okay." I paused to smile at her, remembering the conversation we shared each time we hiked together. "Maybe we'll see a lion."

A glimmer of mischief played in her eyes. "There are no lions here,

Charlie," she replied as she always did.

"Then maybe we'll see a tiger."

"There are no tigers here, Charlie."

"Then maybe we'll see a bear."

"Yes, Charlie, maybe we'll see a bear," she laughed.

The ice was broken and as we entered the tree line, she began speaking without further instigation.

"I need to talk to you about the time travel thing. And I need you to listen to what I'm saying. Not just hearing the words, but actually listening to what I'm going to say." She looked at me sternly as if she was scolding a child. I tried not to smile.

"Okay. Got it. I'm listening."

We walked along the wooded path, our feet crunching the decaying leaves and broken limbs from the oaks towering above our heads. Although the sun managed to weave its way between the branches, it was surprisingly cool on the forest floor as we made our way toward the falls.

"I told you yesterday I think using your trip to find your mother is a bad idea. But the reason I think it's a bad idea isn't because I don't want you to find her. It's because I don't want you using your trip. Not now. Maybe not ever."

"Why in the world not?" I interrupted.

She continued walking straight ahead, carefully maneuvering over tree stumps and animal holes.

"I used my trip, Charlie," she said, stopping midstride to face me.

"You did what?"

"I used my trip. After Branson died. I went back to try and save him." She turned to continue walking, leaving me dumbfounded in the middle of the path. I ran to catch up with her, nearly killing myself tripping on an exposed tree root.

"Tell me everything," I said when I eventually caught up.

She stopped, taking in a deep breath and the courage she needed to go on.

"I missed him. I was lost without him. But I've already told you that a million times before. I just stopped living for a long time. And then one day I got the idea to go back in time and save his life. And that's what I did. Only I wasn't able to save his life, and instead, I ended up making a huge mess of things."

I couldn't believe what she was telling me. My Brooke. Brooke Wallace, the girl who followed rules to a fault, was telling me that she used her one and only trip back in time with the sole intention of changing the past. She'd broken the cardinal rule of time travel.

"So what did you do?" I asked when I finally found my voice.

"I went back again to try and fix what I messed up."

"What!?" I cried. "No one gets two trips!"

She grinned, knowing she'd surprised me. "I did," she said. "I actually got three."

We stopped walking and were now standing in the middle of the woods with only birds and squirrels to eavesdrop on our conversation. I didn't know what to say to her. For the first time in our relationship, I was dumbfounded.

"I kept messing things up and I kept not saving Branson, but finally, on my third trip back, I figured it out."

"You figured what out?"

"I figured out that I don't get to decide what happens in my life. I get to make choices about how I react to the events that transpire, but I don't get to play God. It's not my job." She hesitated. "I could have ruined my whole life, Charlie. I would have, if I hadn't found ways to keep going back. But I was lucky that I eventually realized what I was doing was wrong. And I fixed things."

There was a long pause as I considered the implications of her disclosure.

"And after all that, Branson still died," I said.

She looked at me with great concern, as if she could will me to understand the gravity of what she was saying. "Yes. Branson still died."

I took her hand and we continued walking. Neither of us spoke. I considered the point she was trying to make with regard to my own time travel.

"I won't change anything. I promise," I told her as we finally reached the falls.

She dropped my hand and glared at me. "You didn't listen to a word I said!"

"I did!"

"You didn't! I told you I messed up everything! When I came back, lives were ruined. People died because of changes that I inadvertently made!"

"Branson was going to die anyway," I said.

"No. There was someone else. When I returned from the second trip she died because I changed the past. I didn't have any idea about the seriousness of what I was doing. One little change, Charlie. One little change…" She stopped and looked into my face with such utter desperation I could barely stand to hold her gaze. "I can't lose you," she said finally.

I was taken aback as she finally revealed the real reason she was afraid for me to use my trip.

"Is that what you think? That I'm going to do something in the past that's going to change our future together?"

She dug at the ground with the toe of her sneaker. "Yes," she replied.

"I would never do that! You're the most important thing in the whole world to me."

"You wouldn't mean to do it. I didn't mean to kill Mrs. Cooper. It just happened." She looked up at me. "It could happen, Charlie. You could come back to find that I'm not in your life anymore."

Deep down, in the very bottom of my soul, I knew what she was saying was true. I knew damaging the present was the risk you took when traveling to the past. I hadn't considered losing Brooke as part of the collateral damage of finding my mother. I knew it was a risk I didn't want to have to take.

I took her face in my hands and kissed her fervently on the lips. "Then we'll find another way to learn about my mother," I said.

"Really?" she squealed, her voice rising three octaves as she jumped into my arms.

"Really," I replied. "But I'm going to need your investigative help. We already know there's nothing online about Victoria Weddington. But maybe we can find something on those microfiche of yours."

"Oh, Charlie! I'm so happy you've changed your mind! I was so worried!"

I hugged her to my chest and breathed her in. "I wouldn't lose you for the world," I replied.

CHAPTER FOURTEEN

Brooke and I spent the next week scouring every outlet we could think of for information about the elusive Victoria Weddington. We discovered a few school records from primary and secondary school with her name but nothing more. There were no photographs. No tangible evidence to validate our hunch. However, we finally found something interesting early one morning as we were doing a broad search of college databases. We happened upon a Victoria Weddington who was enrolled at a university in Washington DC around the same time the Victoria we were looking for would have been attending. It appeared, at long last, that we had stumbled upon some useful information. Through the college, we were able to fill out an online request to obtain her transcripts, which included her home address and college ID. Brooke recognized immediately that the ID had nine digits, just like a social security number. The address verified that she was Victoria Weddington, daughter of Representative and Mrs. Weddington. The last piece of the puzzle would be confirming that she was in fact my mother.

Brooke suggested contacting the school's alumni department to see if we could get our hands on a copy of her senior yearbook. The woman I spoke to on the phone was extremely sympathetic to my predicament, and was nice enough to scan and email a copy of the yearbook page with Victoria's photograph. We stood nervously by the computer, waiting for the email to arrive. She refreshed the page repeatedly until at last the subject line 'Weddington' appeared at the top of the email list. Sitting beside her at the computer, I watched the muscles of Brooke's jaw clench involuntarily. I knew she was as anxious for answers as I was. She leaned in front of me to get a better view of the screen as I carefully scrolled the mouse over the attachment and clicked.

In an instant, the photograph of a young woman appeared. She was slightly younger than the image of the girl from the photograph in my father's office that was etched into my mind. But they were one and the same. Of that I had no doubt.

Brooke gasped audibly. "It's her."

I pressed my palm against the computer monitor as if to touch her face. "I can't believe it," I said. "We found my mother."

She wrapped her arms around my waist and pulled me close. "At least now you know. The search is over."

I returned her embrace but did not share her sentiments. To me, it felt as though it was time to begin anew. A dormant torch inside of me was sparked to life. Knowing who she was confirmed the identity of my grandparents, and I was suddenly filled with the desire to find out everything I could about my family.

"I need to call the Weddingtons."

She released her arms and pulled away from me, sitting down on my bed. "Why would you do that? It was clear they didn't want anything to do with you when you showed up on their doorstep. Don't do this to yourself, Charlie."

"Now that I know for sure, I can make them understand. Maybe if I explain they're my grandparents, I'll finally get through to them."

"Charlie, look at you. You're the spitting image of Victoria. You don't think her own mother didn't notice?"

I knew she was right. I saw the recognition in her face. She knew who I was. And she still didn't care. I picked up the football off my bedroom floor and threw it against the wall in anger. Brooke pulled me down to where she was sitting on the foot of the bed and ran her hand against my cheek.

"You promised me you weren't going to get hurt."

"I'm not hurt!" I replied a little too forcefully.

She caressed my bottom lip with her finger. "Liar."

I replayed the conversation I had with Linda Weddington over again in my head. It struck me that I never actually spoke with her husband.

"I need to call Theodore. I need to call my grandfather. Maybe he'll want to talk to me. She never even gave me a chance the other day. She didn't even tell him who it was at the door."

She took a deep breath and laid her head in my lap. "Charlie Johnson, as sure as I'm sitting here, you're going to get yourself hurt."

Brooke left for work before ten, and by lunchtime, I managed to track down three different phone numbers for Representative Weddington. I decided to try his work extension first, to see if I could somehow sneak my way in through the backdoor by claiming to be someone I wasn't, interested in speaking to him as a campaigner. I spent another hour researching his 'hot button' topics, and found he was known to sympathize with hydraulic fracking lobbyists. Knowing I had less than 15 minutes before I needed to get ready for work, I mustered the courage to pick up the receiver. On the third ring, a weary sounding secretary answered the phone.

"Representative Weddington's office. How can I help you?"

I hesitated for a moment, unable to remember what I wanted to say.

"Hello? Is anyone there?" the secretary asked.

Finally, I found my voice. "Yes. Hello. My name is Edward Masterson and I would like to speak with Congressman Weddington about next month's legislation seeking to limit fracking regulations."

"And who can I tell him you're with?"

"I'm calling from the office of the House Natural Resources Committee Chairman," I lied.

"Where can you be reached?"

I gave her my cell phone number.

"I'll give him the message. Have a nice day."

With that, there was a dial tone at the other end of the line.

Four days later, I was in a managers' meeting, discussing our restocking order for the second half of the summer, when my phone rang. I glanced casually at the number to see if it was someone I knew and didn't immediately recognize the number. By the fourth ring, I was getting dirty looks from around the table, and it suddenly dawned on me that the area code was a DC exchange. Frantically, I stood up, knocking my chair on to the floor as I excused myself and ran into the hallway to take the call.

"Is this Edward Masterson?" a woman asked.

"Yes," I replied.

"Hold, please, for Representative Weddington."

Elevator music was piped through the line. I steadied myself against the wall and concentrated on remembering to breathe. I decided I wasn't going to keep up the charade of pretending I was from the Natural Resources Committee. I was cutting right to the chase. At least I hoped I was.

A stern voice startled me from my thoughts. "This is Weddington," he said.

My prepared speech poured out hastily, all in one breath. "Representative Weddington my name is Charlie Johnson and I believe I am your grandson and that my mother was your daughter Victoria."

There was silence on the other end of the line. There was no background noise. No breathing. No sound at all. For a minute, I was sure he'd hung up on me.

"Sir?" I said.

He cleared his throat, still hesitant to speak. Finally, after several more seconds, he responded.

"Mr. Johnson, I would encourage you to stop barking up whatever tree you're looking to climb. I have nothing for you. No information to share. No story to corroborate. Just move on with your life and leave the past in the past." He paused, clearing his throat again. "And as for contacting me again concerning this matter, let me assure you that I will not hesitate to press harassment charges. Are we clear?"

My head was spinning. "Yes, sir."

"Good day then, Mr. Johnson."

"Goodbye," I replied feebly.

I ended the call and slid down the wall onto the floor, burying my head in my hands. The realization that my own grandfather wanted nothing to do with me, officially closing the only means of finding out more about my mother, came as a crushing blow. In that moment, I felt as though I had never experienced such cruelty.

But then I remembered that wasn't the case.

Instances of my father's own heartlessness flooded my mind. The way he spoke about the public behind their backs, ridiculing them for their collective stupidity and inability to care for themselves. The times I saw him turn his back on people who considered him a friend in their time of need. How he told me to 'grow up' when he found me crying alone among the shade trees the day my retriever Greta died.

To have my grandfather treat me with the same harshness was almost more than I could bear. I fought back the mixture of rage and sorrow which threatened to overtake me by closing my eyes and breathing deeply through my nose. After several minutes, I composed myself enough to return to my meeting.

As soon as I was able, I called Brooke to see if she was available after lunch to help me continue searching for my mother. I was directed to her voice mail, confirming she was still at the clinic, where she would probably be for the rest of the day. Without her assistance, I knew it would be difficult to dig up any more information about Victoria, but I was determined to try.

Melody found me hunched over my computer at the kitchen table and offered her assistance. Working together, we began the process of tracking down my mother using the ID number from her college transcript. We were initially excited, as it appeared the ID was in fact her social security number. Unfortunately, after searching for several hours, it didn't yield a single shred of useful information. With every dead end we encountered, our frustration grew.

"Another sealed file," I grumbled, pushing my chair away from the computer screen.

Melody shook her head. "Every record of her has been sealed or has disappeared altogether. It's the strangest thing. How does all evidence of a person's existence just vanish like that?"

I rocked on the two back legs of my chair. "I have no idea. The real question isn't how though. It's why."

She was thoughtful for a moment. "You know, I remember seeing something a few minutes ago that got me thinking. Can we do a search of bank accounts?"

"Maybe," I said, returning to the keyboard. "Let's see."

Within a few minutes, we discovered a bank account tied to her social security number. Someone closed it the month she passed away.

"There's no other information tied to that account. No direct deposit information. No closing balance. Nothing. Another dead end," I said.

"It would be nice to be able to go back and find out more about that account," Melody said.

I sighed. "It would be nice to be able to go back and just talk to her."

She looked at me conspiratorially. "Brooke would freak out."

"She would. She has serious issues with time travel."

"Serious issues," she agreed.

We were silent for a moment while I strummed my fingers fretfully on the keyboard. I grinned at her. "I guess I could try talking to her again."

"She usually gets over things pretty fast."

"This is a pretty big thing, I think."

Melody shrugged. "What's the worst she's gonna do? She's not going to break up with you. She loves you, Charlie. She's just scared of what might happen."

"Nothing's going to happen."

"Exactly. So just tell her that." She stood up to stretch. "Maybe she could go with you."

"That would be a fantastic idea… except she already used her trip."

Melody froze with her arms above her head. "She did what!?"

"I know. I couldn't believe it either. She just told me last week. Apparently, after Branson died, she went back to try and save his life. Not just once. Three times."

"Three times!" she exclaimed as she hoisted herself onto the counter and pulled her knees to her chest. "I would have never guessed she'd have done that. No wonder she's worried."

"No kidding. I wish there was a way to have her there though. I mean, she'll be there, but I won't be able to tell her what I'm doing. She won't be able to help."

She looked curiously at me. "Why not?"

"It's the rules, Mel."

"The rules are that you can't tell anyone in the past that you're using your trip from the future, right?"

"Right."

"But what if she told herself?"

I gazed at her skeptically.

"No, really." She explained, "She could write herself a letter or something. You could take it with you and hide it in the past for her to find. Then you're not telling her. She's telling herself. No rules against that, right?"

It only took me a moment to consider her suggestion before deciding it was one of the best ideas I'd ever heard. I smiled brightly at her.

"If you weren't already my sister, Melody Johnson, I'd adopt you myself!"

Her cheeks flushed crimson. "Do you think Brooke will go for it?"

"If she doesn't, I'm no worse off than I am now. I'll give her a call. Maybe we can go out to dinner tomorrow night and I can ask her."

"Fingers crossed."

"Fingers crossed," I agreed.

CHAPTER FIFTEEN

Since she was coming straight from the veterinary clinic, I decided to meet Brooke at the restaurant. She chose our old standby, Pasta Casa, where we'd shared many bowls of linguini over the years. As I watched her cross the parking lot from the booth where I was seated inside, the comfort of the familiar setting was replaced by anxiety over the proposal I was about to make.

I waved to her as she scanned the dining room, and when our eyes connected, her face lit up just as it had the first time we met. The same way it did every time we reconnected with one another after being apart. I hoped she would light up when I found her in the past, and more importantly, when I returned to her in the present.

"Howdy," she said, collapsing into the booth across from me, still wearing her scrubs.

"Rough day?" I asked.

"We had a dog brought in that was hit by a car this morning. He was in rough shape, poor little guy. Broken leg, dislocated hip. Multiple contusions. Dr. Anderson is a miracle worker though. I think Duke is gonna pull through."

"That's good news."

"It is."

There was a comfortable silence as we both scanned our menus.

"I don't know why I even bother to look as this," she commented, sliding the menu across the table. "I always order the same thing."

"You're nothing if not predictable."

"There's nothing wrong with being predicable." She smiled. "I just like what I like."

"Well, I'm glad you like me," I said, reaching across the table to take her hand.

The waitress arrived to take our orders. I listened to Brooke explaining how she wanted her entrée, with extra vegetables and grated cheese on the side, light on the sauce with rice pasta. I wondered how others perceived her meticulous attention to detail to which I had grown so accustomed. The thought of losing her suddenly filled me with dread, and I nearly changed my mind about discussing my trip. I felt a bead of sweat slowly making its way along my hairline down the side of my face. I decided to speak up before losing my nerve completely.

"I have to talk to you about something," I said.

She took a sip of her water. "I figured. What with the mid-week dinner date and all. So spill. What's up?"

I hesitated briefly before confessing, "I have a plan for finding out about my mother."

"Okay."

"I have a plan about how I can use my trip so you won't be upset."

She looked up from her glass and her skin blanched.

"I have a plan," I repeated, reaching out to take her hands. "Please hear me out."

She didn't say anything for several seconds as she scrutinized me. It was almost as if she was searching for some secret written in the lines of my face. "You said once that the only reason you would ever use your trip would be to find out the truth about your family."

"I did?" I asked, having never remembered saying that to her.

"You did. You just don't remember because it happened during a timeline of which you were never a part."

She wasn't making any sense. I shook my head. "What are you talking about?"

She squeezed my hands and took a deep breath. Her voice wavered when she spoke.

"The day on the quad, playing football together… it wasn't the first time I met you."

"You saw me on campus before?"

"No, Charlie. I met you on one of my trips. We were together. Until we weren't."

She still wasn't making any sense.

"I never planned on telling you any of this. I didn't think it was important for you to know. There was so much pain and I caused so many problems. I just didn't want to subject you to it again. That's why I've never told you."

"Never told me what?!" I exclaimed, causing the family at the table beside us to look in our direction.

"Charlie, the first time I went back, I saw you the day you went to pick up Melody from where she was playing in the lot beside Cooper's Hardware Store. Do you remember that day?"

I did. Vaguely. I nodded.

"I never met you that trip. When you came to get her, I was hidden in the attic of the store. But I saw you through the window, and after that, I couldn't get you out of my mind. When I went back the second time, I returned to Cooper's the same day, hoping I would get a chance to see you again."

"And was I there?"

"Yes."

"And did we meet?"

"Yes."

I was afraid to ask more questions, and yet I needed to know what had become of us during the parallel timeline.

"And did I love you like I love you now?"

A single tear formed in the corner of her eye. She wiped it away before it rolled down her cheek.

"Yes," she whispered.

I walked around the table and slid into the booth seat beside her, wrapping her in my arms.

"I'm so sorry, Charlie," she wept into my shoulder. "I never wanted to hurt you again."

I couldn't believe what I was hearing. The thought of the two of us existing together in some other time, in some other way, was almost more than I could fathom. It suddenly struck me that she had another relationship with me I knew nothing about. I didn't know whether to be angry or envious.

"What happened?" I asked, knowing I didn't necessarily want to hear the answer.

After drying her eyes with a paper napkin, she sniffled several times and composed herself before continuing. "Branson got sick again and I lost it. I got so angry at myself for failing; I alienated everyone, including you and Branson. Even though you told me you'd wait for me to get through it, I broke up with you and that was it."

"But you went back a third time. Didn't you try to fix what happened between us like you fixed everything else?"

"No."

"No?" I was suddenly angry. "Why not?" I asked, raising my voice.

"Because you asked me not to."

She lost herself in a fit of weeping just as our food arrived. She immediately pushed it away, so I asked our server for the bill and to box up our meals. Brooke slipped quietly through the maze of tables, making a beeline for the car, and after paying at the counter, I headed out the door. Once we were alone in the parking lot, she continued her story.

"I went to see you, in the present, after my second trip. I was trying to find a way back again and wanted your help. You were upset with me. Rightfully so. I broke your heart. You told me if I ever did go back a third time, you didn't want to meet me. You didn't want the possibility of going through all the pain again." She rested her head in her hands. "I simply honored your wishes, Charlie. That's why I didn't fix things with you."

So much of our relationship suddenly shifted into focus. The times she knew things about me I'd never shared. Her level of comfort with me when we first met. Her repeated declaration that the universe wanted us to be together.

"You knew me already," I mused.

"Yes."

"But you let us happen again, in our own time, in our own way. You've never interfered. It would have been so easy just to tell me the truth."

She shrugged. "Then it wouldn't have been real for you. You had to fall in love with me on your own, not because I told you to. Besides, you never would have believed me anyway."

"Perhaps," I said, gripping the steering wheel in both hands and focusing on a family coming out of the restaurant.

"So anyway, now you know why I can't let you go back. I got a second chance with you. I'm not willing to risk not getting a third opportunity if something were to go wrong."

"I get it," I said, "but what if there was a way for you to come back with me?"

"I've already been back three times, Charlie. The government will never allow a fourth trip. I just don't see it happening."

"I know. I thought the same thing. But Melody had a brilliant idea. She suggested you write a letter to yourself explaining what's going on. I can take it back with me and hide it for you to find. Once you read it, you'll know what's going on and can help me."

She thought for a moment. "Doing that will change the past, so it will definitely change the future. We don't know how it will turn out for us."

"I think we have a better chance of coming out of this still together if we're both aware of what's going on in the past. It's gonna change either way. I'm going to meet my mother. I have to, Brooke."

She leaned toward me to sweep a strand of hair off my forehead. Her face was red and blotchy, her mascara smeared below her eyes. "Finding your mother really means this much to you?"

I considered her question. My father kept secrets from me my entire life. The secrets prevented us from being close. I knew I was done having secrets in my life. Now I only wanted the truth. I needed to find out the truth about who I was and where I came from. I needed a solid foundation on which to build the rest of my life.

"Yes. It does. But it will mean a whole lot more if I have you by my side."

She let her head fall against the headrest and folded her hands in her lap. "If it's that important to you, then we should do it. You should go meet your mother. And I'll be there to help you do it."

I couldn't believe her change of heart. "Do you mean it?"

"I mean it. I'll write the letter in the morning."

CHAPTER SIXTEEN

It took three months to complete my time travel training and receive my official approval documentation. During that time, Brooke wrote her letter as she promised, and we both returned to school. After her revelation about our previous relationship, it was as if a dam burst and she was no longer able to hold back the secrets she'd been bottling up inside. She told me dozens of stories about our time together during her second trip into the past. Not only about our relationship but also about the relationship Branson and I shared. At first, I was jealous of her for having memories of us I didn't share. But listening to her describe our first kiss, our first hike to the falls, my grandmother's 80th birthday party - I realized how blessed I was to have been given a second chance with her, and my jealousy faded away. Unfortunately, this awareness of just how lucky I was made it all the more difficult to put that second chance in jeopardy by using my trip. I was committed, however, to stay the course.

I tried to rationalize my decision to myself during the course of my traveling education, but there was no rational explanation for what I was feeling or what I was about to do. My mom loved and cared for me with the same devotion she'd shown Melody over the years, and yet, I felt an intrinsic pull toward a woman I didn't remember for a reason I didn't understand.

I decided not to tell my mom about using my trip. Time travel was virtually instantaneous in the present timeline, making it unnecessary to burden her with my decision. Although she supported me in the search for my mother, saying it and accepting it were two very different things. I could see just beneath the surface, it made her sad. She commented offhandedly several times about 'not being enough' for me, and that I might be disappointed with what I eventually found. I knew her remarks came from a place of pain and grief, confirming my decision to keep my trip from troubling her further.

I also began having weekly phone conversations with Dr. Richmond at Brooke's request, part of the trade-off for her helping me in the past. I had no desire to speak with him about my father but found it helpful to discuss how I felt about my adoption. Although we established a strong rapport during the course of our talks, I was still hesitant to tell him about the plans for my trip. Brooke repeatedly assured me he was bound by doctor-patient confidentially laws, and so on the night before my trip, I called him one final time, hoping he would share some insight to help me understand what I was feeling.

"I'm risking the relationships with the people I love here in the present on the off chance I might see my birth mother in the past. That's crazy, isn't it?" I asked.

"What you're feeling isn't crazy, Charlie. It's very common for adopted children to feel isolated and abandoned, even when they've been raised by loving, supportive families. The need for closure is a powerful motivator. It's what's driving your decisions now."

"But why should I care about her at all? I don't know her. She gave me away. She obviously didn't even love me."

"That's just the thing... you don't know her. It's hard for the human spirit to not know, especially about things that make up the very core of who we are. It's natural to want to know who you came from and what your life was like when you were together. Her story is part of your story; a prologue if you will. And your prologue is missing. Our sense of self and self-worth are shaped by so many facets of our lives, and although it seems strange to you that not knowing your birth mother could affect either one, I assure you it is certainly the case for many adopted children." He sighed heavily into the receiver. "It would just be easier if there was another way to get your closure without having to resort to such drastic measures."

"I've tried everything I can think of here. I don't know what else to do. I wish I could just forget about it and move on, but I can't. I've tried, but I feel like if I don't take this opportunity now, I'll never do it. And I know the further I have to travel back in time, the greater the chance of altering my timeline, so it's now or never. I can't stand the thought of never. If I don't take this chance, I might regret it for the rest of my life and I don't think I'd ever forgive myself."

There was silence on the other end of the line.

"Dr. Richmond?"

"You've already made your decision, Charlie. I'm not sure what you're looking for from me. I can't promise you everything will work out. I can't promise you it won't. What I do know is that everyone has to follow their own path and make decisions that feel right to them. I hope you find the answers you're looking for and they give you the peace you're so anxious to find."

His words resonated with me as Brooke drove me to the time travel facility the next morning. As we sat together, waiting for my name to be called, her feet tapped nervously against the grey linoleum.

"It's going to be okay," I said, giving her knee a squeeze. "I'll link up with you as soon as I get there so we can get started right away. I just hope two weeks will be enough time to find her."

"I'm scared," she said. "It's strange for me, being the one left behind, not in control of my own fate. And I know it's stupid that I already miss you so much, especially since you should be back in a few hours. I only have to wait until later in the day, but you have to survive two weeks of not knowing how it will turn out. It's hard knowing I may not be waiting at your house when you return."

"You'll be there, Brooke."

"Unless something goes wrong and everything changes."

"Nothing will go wrong. Everything will be fine. As soon as I'm back, the agent will drop me off at home, and you'll be able to get me up to speed. I'll see you there. I promise."

She massaged her temples with her fingers. "You have the letter?"

"I have the letter."

I reached under her chin, lifting her face to mine, and kissed her tenderly on the lips. "I love you."

"I love you, too," she whispered.

She slid closer, resting her head on my shoulder until my name was called. As she sat up, I knew I needed to move quickly before I changed my mind about going. Without a word, I pecked her quickly on the forehead, and backed away. I didn't take my eyes off her as I made my way into the steel chamber. Behind the glass wall, I saw her crying. My confidence began to waver, and for a moment, I considered walking out. But then I quickly refocused on finding out the truth about my mother. The truth of our time together. The truth my father took to his grave.

I waved goodbye to Brooke. She was saying something, but I couldn't make out what it was. I cupped my hand around my ear and shrugged my shoulders, hoping to convey I didn't hear what she said. She began again, and this time, I was able to read her lips. "I believe in you," she said.

Before I could reply, the door to the chamber was sealed between us. Instructions were piped in through a speaker system and I did as I was told. A timer on the wall counted down the seconds. There was a warm brightness that was nearly blinding, and in an instant, I was back.

PART TWO

CHAPTER SEVENTEEN

As per the traveling instructions, I chose a secluded spot in which to return. Because time travel creates a rift in the timeline which is seen as a bright light on both ends of the continuum, it's necessary to choose somewhere isolated so it won't be visible to anyone else. When the brightness around me faded, I found myself in the center of my bathroom on a rainy Thursday afternoon. I was looking directly at myself in the mirror. It was strange, facing myself as I was in the past. Not much had changed in a year. At least not physically.

I heard voices from below me in the kitchen. There was a man's voice. It was my father.

I promised myself before leaving that I wouldn't discuss my adoption with him. I knew it was going to be difficult not to say the things I wanted to regarding the way he treated me or the secrets he kept. But I knew the less I changed about the past, the better chance I had of maintaining the integrity of the timeline. However, hearing his voice again for the first time since before his death gave me pause, and for a moment, I doubted my ability to keep the peace.

I felt for Brooke's letter to herself in my pants pocket. Incredibly, it remained where I had placed it, inspiring me out of the bathroom and into action. I had no idea how I was able to carry it with me into the past, but Brooke assured me it would work, as she traveled with a tiny clay lion on each of her trips. As always, she was right.

I tried to remember what I'd done on the particular day to which I returned. I was usually lucky if I could remember what I ate for breakfast, so recalling a single day in the summer between my sophomore and junior year of college seemed nearly impossible. During my time travel classes, I was taught that context clues would help me make a smooth transition into the past. As I ventured out of the bathroom, I began having serious doubts about the intelligence of my instructors.

Downstairs, I found Melody engrossed in a novel on the family room sofa, our cat Felix curled up on her lap.

"Hey, Charlie," she said absently as I entered the room.

"Hi." My mind raced. I tried to remember my training. "What do you have going on tonight?" I blurted out.

She peered at me over the top of her book. "I thought I was going to the movies with you and Brooke. Did you change your mind about taking me?" she asked.

Much to my surprise, I immediately remembered some of what happened during the previous timeline. I'd worked the breakfast and lunch shift at the country club, and taken both girls to see an abysmal chick flick that night. We stopped to pick up fast food on the way to the theater where I ate a chicken sandwich, and Melody spilled ketchup on her shorts.

I tried to recover. "Of course not. I just didn't know if something might have changed for you. You and your friends always have impromptu slumber parties popping up out of nowhere. It's hard to keep up!"

"No way. I really want to see *Love Sparkles*. I've been looking forward to it all week."

I suppressed a groan, remembering how much I hated *Love Sparkles*. "Okay. We'll leave in half an hour. I'll treat you to dinner before if you want."

"And Brooke too?" she asked excitedly.

"Yes, and Brooke too."

She closed her book and tossed it on the floor. "I've gotta go get ready. I'll meet you outside."

Dinner went exactly as it had the year before. I ate a chicken sandwich. Melody spilled her ketchup. I smiled as she did it, knowing it was coming. I hoped the majority of the timeline I wasn't planning on changing would be enough to counterbalance the parts that I was. I considered allowing Melody to spill the ketchup a small victory.

After I dropped Brooke off at home, I made the first significant change to the timeline as I placed the letter to herself in her own mailbox. My hands shook as I slid the envelope inside, knowing there was no turning back.

"What was that?" Melody asked as we pulled away.

"Nothing important," I replied. "Just a love note."

She scrunched up her nose as if she smelled something rotten. "Gross," she said.

I chuckled to myself, knowing how her opinion of love would change over the course of the next year.

At lunchtime the following day, my cell phone rang in my pocket as I was reprimanding the kitchen staff about the cleanliness of their stations. I excused myself into the dining room where I immediately checked the caller ID and saw it was Brooke.

For a split second, I didn't want to answer the call. I was scared she was angry. I was nervous she'd be unwilling to help. I was petrified of losing her.

I pressed the call button.

"Hello," I said cautiously.

"Is this real?" she asked, bypassing all formalities.

"Yes."

"So what you're telling me is that a year from now your father is dead, but he's not really your father because you were adopted, and so we've been trying to find your birth mother, but she's dead too, and now you've come back here to find her and you want me to help?"

"Yes."

"Do you have any idea how many problems you've just created for us?!" she screamed at me without raising her voice.

"Yes. You told me." I paused. "You told me everything."

There was dead silence on the other end of the line. I thought for a moment she hung up.

"We have to do this carefully. And you can't tell me stuff like that. That I told you about my trips. You can't tell me anything more about the future than is absolutely necessary. Knowing too much about what's going to happen can ruin both our lives. It's the reason not telling people you're from the future is such an important rule. You remember that section of class?"

"Of course," I acknowledged, remembering the lecture on the dangers of knowing too much and the lives it destroyed.

"And we have to meet during times when we weren't with other people the first time around. If you skip out on lunch with your mom to meet with me, you may be causing something catastrophic to happen in her life. You get that, right?

"Yes."

"So then the best time to do this would be when we were already together, by ourselves, in the initial timeline. I'll only do this with you if we try to minimize changes in other people's lives. Promise me."

"Agreed."

More silence.

"This is crazy," she said.

"Yeah."

"Whose idea was it to come back?"

"Melody's."

"And whose idea was it to use the letter to tell me what was going on?"

"Melody's"

"Smart kid. You're gonna need my help so you don't screw this up."

"I know. That's why we knew I needed to tell you. Or you needed to tell yourself."

She paused again. "You were already coming over tonight to watch the ballgame with my dad, right?"

"Yeah."

"Did you stay for a while after the game last time?"

I smiled, remembering our evening together. "Yes."

"Were we alone?"

"Yes."

She sighed. "Then I guess we can start searching tonight. Try to keep as much as possible the same with my family while you're here before then, okay?"

"Okay." I took a deep breath. "So does this mean you're helping me?"

"Of course I'm helping you," she replied. "What other choice do I have?"

She was right. I hadn't really given her any other options.

"Tonight then?" she asked.

"Yeah," I said. "See you tonight. And Brooke... I love you."

"Love you too," she replied.

It was difficult to carry on a normal conversation with Brooke's dad as we watched the baseball game together. He kept trying to spark discussions about individual player's batting averages, and who should be pulled from the bullpen, and why the team needed a new manager. I remembered our animated dialogue during the first timeline, and tried to recall what I had said before, but unfortunately this time around, baseball was the furthest thing from my mind. By the end of the game, instead of being on the edge of my seat, screaming at the television as I had in the previous timeline, I found myself distractedly watching the clock, despite the fact our team was ahead 3-2 in the bottom of the ninth inning.

As soon as her father excused himself to bed, Brooke curled up beside me on the sofa with her computer propped on her lap.

"Well," I commented offhandedly, "this is a far cry from what we did together after the game last time."

"Oh yeah?" She smiled knowingly at me. "Just what are you making me miss out on?"

"Not internet research, that's for sure," I laughed, pulling her into my arms. "As much as I'd like to focus more on you and less on this, I only have two weeks, so we need to move as quickly as possible. There'll be plenty of time for canoodling once I get back."

"Is that what we spent our time doing? Canoodling?"

"Pretty much."

"That's disappointing," she said. "I feel like I'm getting ripped off."

"Welcome to my world! Now you know how I felt when you told me we had an entire relationship I never knew about!"

"Touché," she said, punching me in the arm. "I guess I can give up a night of canoodling. You owe me though."

"Noted." I kissed her safely on the forehead so as not to cause us any further distractions. "So, can we finally get started?"

"Yes," she replied, pulling up her web browser. "I spent some time alone this afternoon while Mom and Dad were at work and snooped around online for Victoria."

"And?"

"And I found some stuff."

"You did? I can't believe it. There wasn't a trace of her in the future."

"Well, there is now. I found a couple of random pictures of her from high school, and then I found the bank account."

I was puzzled. There hadn't been a single photograph of her when we searched together in the present timeline, but there she was, a very young looking Victoria in front of me on the screen. I took the computer from her.

"What the heck?" I said, tracing her image with my finger. "We never found these. They're gone a year from now."

"You really shouldn't tell me stuff about the future, remember?" She leaned her head back against the sofa and stretched out her legs. "But that is awfully strange."

"Tell me about it. Someone must have taken them down between now and then." I handed her back the laptop. "So what's the deal with the bank account?"

"The deal is it gets money directly deposited into it every month."

"For real?"

"For real."

"How in the world did you get into this? You need a password."

"I had a password."

I shot her a look of disbelief.

"Finding the account was easy using the social security number you gave me. I just cross checked it with all of the large, national banks and it came right up. I cross referenced it with the other information we have on her, and once I knew it was her account, I just started trying passwords. Got in on the third try."

"Don't tell me…"

"VICTORIA1234."

"No."

"Yup."

I stared at her incredulously.

"That was almost too easy. So does it have her address and telephone number?"

"No."

My shoulders slumped.

"I'm sorry," she said. "There's no address. Or phone number. I couldn't find a listing for her anywhere."

"Then we've hit another dead end." I felt a knot forming in my stomach.

"Not necessarily," she said, turning the screen toward me. "Take a look at this rather long deposit and withdrawal history."

I began scrolling down the screen, scanning my mother's account record. Every month, on the first of the month, $1500 was deposited into her account from an unnamed source labeled 'offshore.' Withdrawals were made frequently, in $500 increments, from an ATM in South Carolina. I searched through nine pages of history before turning from the screen.

"How far back does this go?" I asked.

"Eighteen years."

I quickly calculated that I was two years old when my mother began receiving money into the account. The amount had never changed. Every month, on the first of the month, she received $1500. I cringed.

"What do you think all this means?" she asked.

I shook my head. It was throbbing and my nausea continued to grow. "It means someone's been paying my mother off for something since I was two years old. Around the same time my parents adopted me, she started receiving these payments. Something's not right."

"No," she agreed. "Something's not right."

The light-hearted mood we shared only half an hour before was washed away by a wave of suspicion.

"More secrets," I said, unable to keep the frustration out of my voice. "Every time I think we're getting closer to finding some answers, we just end up uncovering more secrets. My father's secrets are still following us around, even now that he's gone."

Brooke reached out to take my hand. "I can't believe he actually died," she said.

"Well, he did. And it's been a real party ever since," I replied, my voice thick with sarcasm.

She hesitated and I could tell that she was gauging my mood. She laid the computer on the floor and crawled into my lap, her legs straddling my hips. The weight of her body immediately grounded me and I pulled her into my chest, grateful for her presence. For a moment, the reality of what I was doing seemed unfathomable, and I imagined if I wished hard enough, I could make all my troubles simply disappear.

"So what should we do now?" she asked finally.

I considered our options. With the help of her research, we finally identified where my mother was living. We also knew each time a deposit was made into her account, she showed up to the ATM at her local branch to make a withdrawal within 48 hours.

The first of the month was only two days away.

"You up for a road trip?" I asked her.

CHAPTER EIGHTEEN

Twenty minutes into our drive south on I-85, neither of us spoke. I knew Brooke was nervous about diverting from the original timeline in order to make the trip to South Carolina. Although we vowed not to spend time away from the people we were with the first time around, when we discovered my mother living so far away, she couldn't stand the idea of being left behind. She changed her mind 15 times before deciding at last to join me, but in order to minimize the impact on the timeline, she only took two days off work. We also decided to reserve a rental car for her to drive back in the event my mother didn't make an appearance by the time she needed to return home.

Even with meticulous planning, her furrowed brows revealed her anxiety, and after nearly half an hour of silence, the droning hum of the tires on the asphalt began to drive me insane.

"It's going to be okay," I said reassuringly, reaching over to tuck a tendril of hair behind her ear.

"I hope so," she said without tearing her gaze from the sea of lodgepole pines out the window.

"You'll see. Nothing catastrophic is going to happen because we aren't where we were the first time around. You said yourself your parents have been working long hours. I'm pretty sure it was just the two of us these two days the last time. Have a little faith, huh?"

I studied her profile as she continued to stare out the window. There was a sadness etched in the lines of her face that had been there since the day I met her. Only after learning about her trips did I come to appreciate that the artist behind those lines was an unbelievably tragic series of events which included more heartache than any one person should have to endure. As the sun poured through the window, transforming her hair from chestnut to the color of a newly minted penny, it occurred to me that I'd never seen her looking more beautiful.

"I'm scared," she said.

There was nothing I could say or do to convince her that our timeline would be unchanged when I returned to the present day. It was a testament to her love for me that she had even agreed to come along to find my mother. I knew how difficult it was for her to risk making changes after everything she'd been through in her own life, and I was suddenly overcome with pure adoration. I didn't deserve her and I knew it.

"Brooke?"

She turned to face me, hearing the concern in my voice. "Yeah?"

"Marry me."

For a moment, she was in total shock, as if a rug had been pulled from beneath her and she was now struggling to regain her footing. As I watched her recover, a series of emotions - disbelief, joy, and excitement, flitted like a movie projection across her face. I was discouraged to see the emotion she settled on was fear.

"Are you serious?" she cried. "You can't ask me that! Not now! Not here in the past! You're going to change everything!"

"I can't help it," I replied. "I love you. I want to be with you. Forever."

She hesitated but a small smile played at the corners of her mouth. "You do?" she asked, softening.

"Yes. I do."

She considered me from the passenger's seat and leaned over to kiss me curtly on the cheek.

"I love you too, Charlie. But we can't have this conversation now. Maybe when you get back. But not now. You're just going to have to be willing to put this topic on a shelf until later. Can you do that?"

I looked at her. She was grinning now. Smiling for the first time in four days. It was a beautiful sight.

"So is that a yes?" I asked.

She punched me in the arm. "If you want your answer, you're going to have to make sure I'm still around when you get back so I can give it to you. That means no more craziness!"

"So I get an answer when I get back?"

"If you haven't ruined everything with your pigheadedness, then yes."

"Fair enough," I said.

We drove in silence for several miles, but I felt pure joy radiating from her side of the car as we continued on our journey south. I stole a glance at her out of the corner of my eye, and knew immediately that I didn't have to wait for my answer until I got back. My answer was written all over her face.

Our stomachs were growling by the time we stopped the car a few miles short of the Georgia border. We found a fast food restaurant just off the interstate and ordered from the drive thru so we could take our food to recon the bank before it got too late.

We pulled up across the street from the address listed on Brooke's GPS and parked in a side lot.

"That's it," she said, nodding toward the bank entrance.

I stared at the nondescript front door flanked by two decorative urns. The bank could have been any bank, in any town across the country. But it wasn't just any bank. It was special. It felt almost sacred as I watched patrons coming and going through the entrance. I knew the only person on earth who held the knowledge of my past would be coming to this particular bank, and as we got out of the car and crossed the busy four lane street, I approached it with reverence.

The ATM was on the corner of the building, facing the opposite street. There was no line, and I strolled by casually in an attempt to keep from drawing attention to myself. However, as I passed before it,

I felt as though it was pulling me in. I stopped and tentatively touched the screen.

"She comes here all the time, Brooke. My mother, Victoria Weddington, uses this very ATM to withdraw the money from whatever benefactor sends it to her."

She wrapped her arms around my waist.

"And she's not dead yet. She's still alive here in the past." I took a deep breath, reflecting on the enormity of what I was hoping would transpire in the days to come. "I might meet her tomorrow."

"What are you going to say?"

I took her hand and walked with her back to the car. The truth was I had no idea what I was going to say. When we began searching for her, the idea of having a conversation with the woman who gave birth to me seemed much simpler. Now, however, the entire journey had become extraordinarily complicated. Because she passed away, I knew once I returned to the present timeline, there would be no follow-up reunion. No family dinner. No holiday celebration with her grandchildren someday. This one encounter would be the only one I would get. I knew I had to make it count.

There was also the matter of her physical and mental condition. My mom made it quite clear that the reason the state allowed for my adoption was because my mother was deemed unfit to parent. I didn't know whether she'd gotten clean and sober over the years, or whether she would be too strung out to even hold a conversation, when and if we found her.

"I guess I'll just introduce myself, and ask if she would like to sit down for a cup of coffee or something. I don't know what I'll do if she says no. I haven't really considered that an option. But I guess she could be like her parents and want nothing to do with me."

She squeezed my hand tightly. "She'll talk to you, Charlie. She'll have to. Now you're the one who has to have some faith."

As soon as we left the bank, we checked in to a small bed and breakfast on the outskirts of the sleepy, southern town. The owners greeted us at the door, offered us chilled glasses of sweet tea, and showed us to the 'peach room' we would be calling home for the night. We were informed that breakfast was served between seven and nine, and that a certain level of decorum was expected from the patronage. Brooke broke into a fit of giggles as soon as the door shut behind us.

"There is to be no horseplay in the hallways," she said, mimicking the older gentleman's southern drawl as she threw herself across the four poster bed.

"You must really look like trouble with the extensive list of rules he felt the need to recite," I laughed.

"Me!" she cried, throwing a pillow in my direction.

"Yes, you!" I replied as the pillow whizzed past my head, nearly knocking a lamp from the dresser. "This is exactly the tomfoolery he's expecting out of the likes of you!"

She grabbed my arm and pulled me playfully onto the bed. "Tomfoolery, huh?"

"Yes," I said, pinning her beneath me and bringing my lips to hers, "tomfoolery."

Her mouth was soft and warm and she returned my kiss willingly. Her hands were on my chest as if to hold me at a distance, and yet I knew that was not her intent. Slowly, she slipped her arms beneath mine and pulled me closely into her embrace, kissing me with increasing desire. She let her hands explore the ridges and valleys of my body, and allowed me to do the same to her. It was a familiar and comforting dance we'd choreographed together over the years, as simple and complex to us as it was to all lovers who came before and to all those who would follow. Through the course of our relationship, we spent many an evening together, holed up in her dorm room, wrapped in each other's arms. As it was on those nights, it proved again, in the dim light of the peach room with its tiny floral wallpaper, to be my very favorite place.

"Charlie?" she said.

"Yes?"

She was curled against my body and the back of her head was resting against my cheek. Tiny wisps of hair tickled my nose and I smoothed them with the back my hand. I waited patiently for her to continue. Finally she spoke.

"Did you mean it?"

"Mean what?" I asked, feigning ignorance, although I knew exactly to what she was referring.

"Mean it about wanting to marry me?"

I chuckled softly and rolled her over so I could see the expression on her face. She was glowing.

"I thought we weren't talking about this," I said with a smile.

"We're not. You're right. Never mind." She rolled back over and slid as far across the bed as she could without falling off the edge. I couldn't resist. I pushed her gently with my foot, and she went tumbling onto the floor with a loud thud.

"You jerk!" she cried, catapulting herself off the floor and tackling me where I was still lying on the far side of the bed. I pinned her arms to her sides and held her on top of me so she was forced to look me in the eyes.

"I meant what I said. I want to be with you. More than anything else in the world."

She considered me skeptically. "We're so young, Charlie."

"We won't always be young. So you don't have to marry me now. You can marry me when you're older."

She laughed. "I'll be older when you get back."

"I think your future self may still think you're too young. She's really practical that way."

"Glad to know I'm still pragmatic in the future."

"To a fault," I teased.

"You shouldn't be telling me that."

I finally released the grip on her arms once I was sure she wasn't going to haul off and slug me for pushing her off the bed. She announced that she wanted to get ready for bed, and after we both finished brushing our teeth, she turned off the lights and snuggled up beside me under the thin cotton sheet.

"Do you think she'll show up?" she asked in the darkness.

I hadn't thought about my mother since leaving the bank.

"I hope so."

"Me too," she said. "Me too."

CHAPTER NINETEEN

After stuffing ourselves on raspberry jam smothered crescent rolls and mini quiches for breakfast, we drove across town to the parking lot beside the bank. Brooke was content to occupy herself with one of the many downloaded books on her tablet. I, on the other hand, was unable to concentrate on any of the games on mine. Every other minute, anxiety compelled me to scan the sidewalk surrounding the ATM for my mother. I drummed my fingers on the steering wheel nervously and eventually tossed the tablet onto the dashboard in frustration.

"Why don't you get out of the car and walk around a bit," Brooke suggested. "You're a mess."

I grunted at her as I continued searching the faces of the pedestrians strolling the block. My stomach growled. I checked my watch and saw it was almost lunch time. "Are you hungry?" I asked.

"Sure," she replied, turning off her tablet. "How about if I go grab something for us to eat? You can stay here just in case she shows up."

Brooke headed off in the car to a sandwich shop across town, leaving me alone with my thoughts in the parking lot. I shuffled along with my hands in my pockets, rehearsing the script I prepared in the event I should meet Victoria. The morning sun reached its peak, and I sought the shade of a mature oak growing out of a hole in the sidewalk. I rested against the trunk and closed my eyes, imagining the warmth of my mother's embrace. However, I knew better than to romanticize her and quickly pushed the thought from my mind. Letting my imagination run would only serve to disappoint me in the end. Several minutes later, Brooke returned, and I ran to join her at the car. She bought a turkey club for each of us and a large bag of chips to share. As I sat with her, staring across the street, mindlessly munching chip after chip, a woman came around the corner, catching my eye. In addition to her frailness, she was overdressed for the summer heat, wearing a long sleeved oxford and oversized hat far too large for her emaciated frame. She walked with a distinct lack of confidence, checking repeatedly over her shoulder as she made her way toward the ATM.

"I think I see her," I whispered to Brooke.

She looked up from her lunch and surveyed the scene. "The one with the hat?"

"Yeah." I stopped breathing. "Should I get out?"

She took my hand. It was cool to the touch. "I guess so. Do you want me to come?"

I considered her for a long moment, as an unspoken understanding passed between us. I knew I had to get out. And I knew I had to do it alone.

"I'm good," I said finally. "Just promise me you'll be here waiting when I get back."

I jogged across the busy street, and watched from a distance as the woman cautiously approached the ATM. She touched the screen and seconds later retrieved her money from the machine. She hastily folded the bills, placed them in her pocket, and began walking down the sidewalk in my direction. I was still unable to see her face clearly, so I continued walking toward her. Thinking about the reality of her proximity, I felt a disconnect between my head and my body, bringing on a sudden bout of vertigo. I braced myself on the side of the building and tried to calm my breathing. The street sounds became static, and the only thing I was aware of was the steady pulse in the artery of my neck. As she passed in front of me, I was finally able to see her features beneath the tattered straw hat.

I fell into step beside her.

"Victoria?" I said.

She turned. Her eyes were glassy. Bloodshot. Hollow. And yet, when she finally allowed herself to focus on my face, I saw them fill with wonder like the eyes of a child. She lifted the brim of her hat and took a step closer; peering at me cautiously the way a hiker would approach a coiled snake.

"Do I know you?" she asked.

I hoped she couldn't hear my heart pounding in my chest. "Not anymore. But I think you did once."

She reached her hand toward my face, as if she intended to touch me. "What's your name?" she asked.

"It's Charlie. Charlie Johnson."

She shook her head and began walking in the opposite direction. As I watched her ambling down the street, I couldn't move. I couldn't speak. I couldn't believe I'd come so far only to find she was as unwilling to speak to me as her parents were. And yet, I knew I'd risked too much to let her continue to walk away. I couldn't allow her to disappear with her secrets. As she rounded the corner, I finally found the courage to call after her.

"Please wait! I have something I need to ask you!"

She froze in place, although she did not turn around.

"He changed your name," she called back over her shoulder. "Your name was Andrew."

Filled with adrenaline, I ran to catch up with her where she remained standing in the middle of the sidewalk. We stood facing one another and it was nothing like how I imagined meeting her would be. But it was exactly how it was supposed to be.

"Is there somewhere we can go to talk? Can I buy you a cup of coffee? Or something to eat?" I asked.

Her eyes darted wildly up and down the street, as if she was waiting for something catastrophic to happen. "Yeah," she said. "There's a place. Follow me."

I turned toward the car and saw Brooke watching me from the passenger's seat where I left her. I waved to her, signaling that I'd be back. She blew me a kiss and held up her hands, fingers crossed.

Ten minutes later, I was sitting across the booth from her at the only fast food restaurant within walking distance. I bought her a large value meal which she wasted no time devouring. I studied her while she ate in silence, ketchup collecting at the corners of her mouth. Her eyes were sunken and dark. The youthful glow captured in the photo from my father's office was gone, replaced by an aura of hopelessness. Her hair was thinning and matted to the top of her head. Despite it all, I could still make out the beautiful woman she had once been.

"So you know who I am?" I asked cautiously.

She popped a fry in her mouth and used a napkin to wipe her face.

"You're my son, Andrew Weddington," she replied matter-of-factly. "How'd you find me? Did your jerk of a father finally tell you the truth about what he did to me?"

I was taken aback by her frankness and lack of emotion. I couldn't respond. I held onto the Formica table with both hands to keep the room from spinning.

She ate another fry. "I'm surprised he let you come see me."

I took a deep breath. "He doesn't know I'm here."

She looked up from what remained of her burger. "He never wanted you to see me again."

"Well, I don't really care what he wants these days. What matters is that I wanted to meet you so you could tell me the truth about where I come from. I tried asking your parents, but they refused to speak to me."

What came out of her sounded less like laughter and more like the cackle of a deranged lunatic. The laughter threw her into a fit of coughing that left her doubled over.

"Are you okay?" I asked.

She smiled. "Oh, yeah. I'm good. Just glad to know some things never change." She returned to her fries.

My heart sank. I couldn't imagine what kind of mother would be able to sit face to face with the son she hadn't seen in two decades and be more interested in the food, which she continued to shovel into her mouth. I knew immediately there'd been tragedy in her life. It was the only explanation for the hardness of her heart.

I cleared my throat. "Will you tell me what happened?"

She took a sip of her soda. "With what? With your dad?"

I didn't understand why she seemed to be obsessing over him. "Sure. But do you mean my biological father or the man that raised me?" I asked.

She grinned at me from across the booth. "He never told you, did he?"

"Never told me what?"

"The man who raised you… the big shot politician, Phil Johnson?" She paused for dramatic effect. "He *is* your daddy."

The pungent smell of grease from the kitchen was overwhelming. I could feel the turkey club I ate for lunch forcing its way into my esophagus, and I swallowed hard to prevent the nausea from overtaking me. I knew I wasn't going to like whatever my mother was going to tell me, but I'd come too far to leave without the answers I deserved.

"Tell me everything," I said. "I need to know what happened. From the beginning."

My mother took the last bite of her sandwich and washed it down with a large gulp of soda. She brushed off her hands and sat back in the booth to begin her story.

"Let's see. It was the summer after my senior year in college. I went back home to apply for a teaching position in the county. I was gonna be a teacher. Can you believe that?" She shook her head and laughed feebly. "Anyway, my parents always held these big summer parties for all their hoity-toity friends, and I'll never forget the night I saw Phil Johnson standing on my parents' balcony for the first time. He was the most handsome man I'd ever seen. The next thing I knew, my father was introducing us. It was like a dream come true." She paused, distracted by something over my shoulder. I turned to see what drew her attention and saw two police officers entering the restaurant. I wondered if she thought they were coming for her.

She slouched in the booth and continued quietly. "That night, he asked me to go with him to a fourth of July picnic the next day. I still remember wearing that gingham yellow sundress. He was such a gentleman. Held the door for me. Stayed by my side, introducing me to all of his friends as his new girlfriend. It was a whirlwind courtship to say the least. We were inseparable after that day.

"As it turned out, Phil was running for city council. Election season was heating up and my father's endorsement won him the election. I was so happy for him." She took another sip of her soda. "Then he broke up with me three days later. Something about not having time for a relationship." She sighed. "Too bad I was already pregnant with you.

"The thing was, I didn't realize I was pregnant for a long while. There weren't any of the typical signs women talk about. I finally went to the doctor because I couldn't figure out why I was so tired all the time, and that's when I found out. By that point, there was no option but to have you, and I panicked. I didn't know what to do, so I went to Phil. He refused to see me. Wouldn't answer my calls. He'd written me off and I knew it." She took a deep breath, and I could see there was more than addiction ruining her life. Pain chained her to the past.

"With nowhere else to go, I told my father. I hoped he'd be supportive. I prayed he would help me. But he wasn't and he didn't. He threatened to go after Phil, but I lied and told him he wasn't the father. I told him there were other men. Of course there weren't, but I knew he could destroy Phil, and for some stupid reason, I still loved the bastard.

"My father kicked me out of the house, calling me a disgrace to the family, and said I could return when I'd 'taken care of my mess.' He told me he wouldn't have my 'indiscretions' ruining his political career, and that he would arrange for me to live at a convent about an hour away until the baby was born. There was an orphanage associated with the nunnery, and I was instructed to put you up for adoption. I intended on doing just that, until the moment you were born."

For the first time since approaching her in the street, my mother looked directly into my eyes. I knew instinctively, every word she said was true. I also knew, in that moment, that I loved her.

"The first time I held you, I knew I couldn't give you away. The nuns allowed me to stay for a few months after you were born, but eventually, they told me I needed to leave. A convent wasn't a place to hide, they said. So I left but knew I couldn't go back home. Not with you. I had no job. No money. Nowhere to live and a baby to take care of. So I just started heading south." She wiped her eyes with the back of her hand as the emotional drain of dredging up the past took its toll. "I tried, Andrew, I tried. I did the best I could. But it was too hard. Way too hard. I met some people who said they'd help me. They gave me my first hit of coke. It was the beginning of the end."

It struck me that our lives were remarkably similar. We were both raised by heartless, tin men, more interested in their political careers than fostering the love of their children. I cautiously reached across the table to take her hand. Her tears were flowing freely now, and she no longer bothered wiping them away.

"I loved you, Andrew... or it's Charlie now I guess. I loved you more than I have ever loved anyone else in my life. But I was broken. I *am* broken. And the drugs, they helped me feel... less broken. I started needing them to get through the day. But there was no money for drugs. And there was no money for taking care of you. So I finally went back to the only person I thought might help me. I went back to Phil."

She pulled her hand away and straightened herself in her seat. A defiant demeanor washed over her as she continued. "He was easy to find. After he won the city council seat, he set his sights on county commissioner and his campaign posters were everywhere. When I confronted him on the sidewalk in front of his office about child support payments, he brushed me aside, threatening me with claims of harassment. Halfway home, having gone over his hateful words a dozen times in my head, I turned the car around and went back. I knew there was no excuse for the way he was treating me, and the only way I was going to get through to him was to fight viciousness with viciousness. I marched into his office and demanded that he see me. I told him I would prove his paternity and go public with the scandal if he didn't pay me off. Without any further baiting, he agreed to directly deposit money into an account as long as I signed a contract swearing I'd never tell anyone about our relationship." She stopped speaking and held her head in her hands. She pulled at her hair nervously, as if she wanted to continue, but couldn't bring herself to go on.

"It's okay," I said, reaching across the table.

She looked up at me with an expression like that of a wounded animal. "He wanted more than just my silence," she whispered. "You were part of the arrangement. He wanted to be sure I could never use you against him."

She buried her face in her arms as she laid her head on the table. Although haggard beyond her years, she appeared more like a child than an addict, and at that moment, I was compelled to slide onto the bench beside her. I wrapped my arms around her shoulders as she began beating her head against the table.

"Mom," I said calmly, "please stop. Don't hurt yourself."

She picked her head up, and her eyes pierced through me. "Did you just call me Mom?"

I hadn't realized my slip. "I guess I did."

She continued to scrutinize me, tears streaking the layer of dirt on her face. "With everything I've just told you, all of the horrible things I did, I don't deserve to be called anyone's mom."

"It doesn't matter what you did. You're still my mother."

"No!" she cried. "I gave you away! I let him have you because I needed the drugs more than I needed to be saddled with a child. I'm nobody's mother. I'm a waste."

She succumbed to a fit of hysterics while I cradled her in my arms. I was struck by the irony of the situation. How I was now consoling the one who should have been caring for me my entire life. I became increasingly agitated as I sat there, smoothing my mother's hair the same way I consoled Melody over the years. By the time Victoria calmed down, I was furious, and she immediately sensed my anger.

"Please don't be mad at me, Charlie. I hoped I was giving you a better life. My world was no place for a little boy."

I held her at arm's length to be sure she could see me fully. "I'm not angry with you. How could I be angry with you? He's the one I'm angry at. I'm angry at my father." I stopped as the extent of my realization washed over me. Phil Johnson was in fact my biological father. There was no one else out there waiting to meet me. No one looking to welcome me into their open arms. There was only a heartless excuse for a father who ended up dead in the bottom of a ravine.

And within a few months, my mother would be dead as well.

A lump rose in my throat, and I knew it was time to leave. I needed to be with Brooke. I needed to sort through the maelstrom of feelings swirling around inside of me. I had no intention of returning to the present without seeing my mother again to say goodbye, but for the moment, I could no longer stand to be so close.

I walked her to the corner. She refused to let me see her safely home. I doubted there was actually a house where she was headed. We agreed to meet again, several days later, at the same restaurant for lunch.

I already knew it would be the last time I'd ever see her.

CHAPTER TWENTY

As I came around the side of the bank, I saw Brooke, still sitting in the passenger's seat of my car in the parking lot where I left her. The window was down and she was reading, the sun illuminating the side of her face. I could almost imagine the warmth of her skin on my hand. The crunch of gravel under my sneakers alerted her to my presence. She looked up from her tablet and relief spread across her face.

"Well?" she asked anxiously as I slid into the car.

I inhaled and held my breath for several seconds before slowly letting it out. I shook my head in disbelief over what had just transpired.

"You want the long version or the short version?" I asked as I started the car.

"The long version. Definitely the long version," she replied.

After sitting in the claustrophobic fast food restaurant for the better part of the afternoon, I couldn't stand the thought of being cooped up. I remembered seeing a sign for a park on the edge of town. Within several minutes, I found my way to the entrance. At the end of the road was a beautiful lake complete with a public pier. There were clouds rolling in, shading the brutal afternoon sun and making the end of the pier a pleasant place to talk. As we sat together, our bare feet dangling over the edge, I told her my mother's story.

"I don't know what to say," she said when I finished. "I would have never guessed your father could have done something like this."

"That's funny," I jeered. "I was thinking just the opposite. This is *exactly* the kind of thing I can imagine him doing. He never hesitated to use people for his own political gain. I've watched him sidle up to dozens of people just long enough to use them before leaving them high and dry. If you didn't serve a purpose in his political life, he'd drop you in a second. He needed my mother's connection to Weddington to ensure he would win the election. When he didn't need her anymore, he left."

"He broke her heart."

"Of course he did. Can you imagine being left alone and pregnant by your boyfriend without any support from your family?"

"No," Brooke said, shaking her head. "Your poor mother. It's no wonder she became an addict. I'm sure she was self-medicating severe depression. It's so common."

"Well, for being an addict, she was surprisingly lucid today. She did have a couple wild swings of hysteria and it got hard to have a conversation with her." I paused, remembering how despondent she seemed. "I guess you were right all along. I really am lucky she gave me away. As awful as my father was, my mom was always amazing. Can you imagine what my life would have been like if I would have stayed here with my mother instead?"

"You'd be just like her. Or worse."

I watched a family of mallards paddling across the lake and allowed the truth of her observation to set in.

"I'm glad I came," I said finally. "It feels better, just to know the other side of the story. Her side. I just wish I could do something to help her."

"You can't help her, Charlie. The damage has already been done."

Her voice was cold. Hard. I strained to see the compassion in her face. "She's gonna die, Brooke."

"I know."

"There's gotta be something I can do to help."

She threw a rock from the pier into the water. "Ugh! Charlie! You can't help her! What don't you understand? You'll change the whole future if you do!" She stood up and started toward the car, throwing her arms in the air. "I knew this was going to happen!"

"You knew what was going to happen?" I called after her.

"I knew after you met her that you were going to want to save her. But you can't, Charlie. You just can't. You have to let her die."

"Says the woman who went back in time three times to try to save her brother's life!"

She froze mid-stride. "Don't you dare bring my brother into this, Charlie," she snapped without turning to face me.

I caught up and grabbed her by the shoulder, spinning her in my direction. "It's not so easy, is it? Letting someone die. You act like it should be no big deal, but you couldn't do it either."

"But I did!"

"Only because you weren't smart enough to figure out how to stop it from happening."

She glared at me and I regretted the words the moment they left my mouth. She pulled out of my grasp and began running toward the car.

In a moment of emotional weakness, I hurt her. The one person I needed to be on my side more than anyone else. I shuddered to think how the pain I caused would trickle forward to change the present timeline. I couldn't risk any more damage. I made it to the car just as the first roll of thunder echoed across the lake. She leaned against the hood, refusing to look at me, her arms crossed defiantly atop her chest.

"I'm sorry," I said as I approached her. "I'm a jerk. It's been a hard day."

Another clap of thunder, accompanied by lightning, boomed over our heads. She didn't respond.

"Brooke, I didn't mean it. I know I can't help her. I know she has to die. But knowing it and accepting it are two different things." I felt a raindrop. "Please. Don't be angry."

She lifted her face. I couldn't tell where the tears ended and the rain began. "You're right," she said. "I tried and tried and tried. And I would have been happy to save him that last time. But I learned my lesson. And I know there's a reason he's not with me anymore. And there's a reason your mother isn't going to be around for you either. I don't know what that reason is, but I do know you can't save her now because we have a future together. A future I hope you're not willing to sacrifice."

The rain began to fall in earnest. She still hadn't budged from the hood of the car or conceded forgiveness. "I'll leave it be, Brooke, I promise. I'll let her go."

"And what about your father? What happens tomorrow when you come face to face with him, knowing what you know now?"

I hadn't considered that I was going to have to confront my father with the newfound information about how he treated my mother. It was going to be hard to keep my mouth shut.

Or keep from punching him in the face.

"Look me in the eye and tell me you're not going to say anything to him," she cried over the din of the storm.

I turned away, running my hands through my hair that was now soaked with rain and dripping down my face. What had I gotten myself into? I didn't know if I was strong enough to do what needed to be done to assure my future would remain unchanged. I stood in the pouring rain, the storm within more volatile than the storm above.

Suddenly, Brooke's arms were around my waist. I wasted no time turning to face her. She was drenched. Soaked through to her skin. Long trails of mascara washed down her cheeks.

"I'm sorry," she said.

I hated that she was the one apologizing when I was the one messing everything up.

"No," I replied, "I'm sorry. I can do this. I found the answers I was looking for and now all that's left is to go home and be a better man than my father was."

She grabbed the back of my head with both hands and pulled me close, kissing me desperately. I felt the heat rising from her lips as the cool rain continued to fall.

"You already are a better man," she said when she released me at last.

On the drive back home that night, I decided not to tell her about my plan to see my mother again before returning to the present timeline. I didn't want her to worry about me endangering our future by making a reckless mistake. I was counting on the fact that I could sneak safely away while she was at work, and she would never know the difference. I knew, despite the risks, I couldn't leave without seeing my mother one last time.

Chapter Twenty One

I underestimated how difficult it was going to be to live under the same roof with my father once I knew the physical and psychological torment he caused my mother for so many years. Finally knowing the truth, I found it was nearly impossible to conceal my anger when I was around him. Thankfully, there were only a few days left before my scheduled return to the present. In the meantime, I avoided him at all cost, working around the clock and spending as much time with Brooke as she would allow. On the few occasions I was forced to interact with him, I bit my tongue and smiled dutifully. There was some concern that I wouldn't be able to keep up the charade for the remainder of the timeline until his death, but Brooke assured me she would help to keep the version of myself that stayed behind in check after my transfer to the present timeline was complete.

Her traveling expertise was invaluable, given the fact that very little was discussed in class about the time between extraction from the past and return to the present. It was assumed that you wouldn't be changing anything during your trip, and therefore your past-self would have nothing to adjust for in the days, months, or even years until you reconnected with yourself in the future. You would just relive the timeline as you did originally and your memories of that time would mirror the actual events of the augmented timeline.

Brooke explained that in addition to being fully aware of the changes she made on her trip, she also retained the memories of the original timeline during each of her trips, but could not account for the time between her extraction and return to the present because there were so many differences. However, it seemed as though the consciousness that remained to live out the remainder of the augmented timeline was fully aware of the changes and relived the timeline accordingly. She explained that I would have no memory of those months when I eventually caught up to myself. I would have to rely on her to fill me in on everything.

The five hour drive south to see my mother again was a lot less fun without Brooke's playful banter. I spent the time ruminating upon why my father had been so motivated to protect the secrets surrounding my birth and adoption. It dawned on me, as I crossed the North Carolina border, that if word had gotten out regarding his treatment of my mother, it would have been a death sentence for his fledgling political career. Everything always came back to his career.

I was irritable and exhausted by the time I pulled into the restaurant parking lot. Without any way to communicate with her, I half expected my mother to have forgotten about our plans, but as I pushed through the double doors, I spotted her immediately, sitting in the same booth we shared earlier in the week.

Unlike our first encounter when I had a specific agenda, as I approached her this time, I knew all I wanted was to get to know more about her before she passed away. I assumed her death would be somehow related to her drug abuse, caused by an overdose, homelessness, or associated violence. It made me sad to think of how different her life would have been if she had never met my father. And yet, I realized if they had never met, I would have never been born.

"Hi, Mom," I said, as I slid into the booth across from where she was sitting.

"Charlie," she said with a crooked smile, "you're here."

"Of course I'm here. How are you?" I asked.

She fidgeted in her seat, wrapping a length of her hair around her dirty finger. The corner of her eye twitched violently.

"I'm fine, Charlie. Just fine." She looked away.

Although she seemed just as coherent as she'd been earlier in the week, I could tell she was nervous. Perhaps the stress of our meeting was too much for her to handle without getting high. I didn't want to agitate her further, so I racked my brain for a topic we could discuss that would be benign enough to settle her frazzled nerves.

"Did you ever have a pet growing up?" I asked.

She stared at me as if I was growing a second head right before her eyes. She blinked twice. Three times. Finally she began.

"I had a bird. His name was Jonathan. Named him after the author of some book I liked as a kid. I don't even remember what it was now."

"Jonathan Swift? He wrote Gulliver's Travels."

"Yeah." She nodded. "I think that was it. Anyway, I wanted a dog. Asked for one every birthday. Christmas too. You name it. But my mother swore she was allergic. Finally, on my ninth birthday, Daddy bought me a grey parakeet." She pulled at another length of hair and looked nervously around the room. "I taught that stupid bird to talk, just to have somebody to talk to. He was pretty cool to have around, but he wasn't the same as a dog." Her chin dropped and she bowed her head. "I haven't thought about Jonathan in a long time. And I never did get my dog."

"I had a dog once," I offered hesitantly.

"You did?" She smiled. "Tell me all about him."

"I was pretty lonely when I was a kid too. I have a sister, Melody, but she wasn't born until I was eight. So for a long time, I was alone. One afternoon, when I was in first grade, my mom…" I choked on the word, hoping I didn't upset her by using it to refer to someone else.

"It's okay," she said. "She's more of a mother to you than I ever was. Go on. Don't stop. Tell me about the dog."

I began again. "One day, my mom picked me up after school and took me to a farm on the other side of town. There were three puppies hiding under a wooden bench. I picked the smallest one, a rambunctious golden retriever. I named her Greta."

"Greta," she repeated. "I like that."

"I spent a lot of time with her. I went to a private school and didn't really know any of the kids who lived around me, so Greta was my playmate. She was a good dog. Loyal. Gentle."

"She sounds a lot like you," my mother said.

I didn't know how to interpret her compliment. It made me uncomfortable to think that I was never really going to know my mother. And she was never really going to know me either. I only wished we had more time.

"I'm hungry. I bet you are too," I said. "Let me go get us some lunch."

I ordered meals for both of us, with extra fries and dessert for her. She was ravenous, just as she'd been the time before. I decided to try and find out more about her life, and in the process, perhaps determine the cause of her death.

"Can I ask you a question?"

"Sure," she replied through a mouthful of fries.

"Where do you live?"

"Here in town."

"No, I mean, do you have a place where you stay?"

"You're asking if I live in a house?"

"Yes," I replied, embarrassed by the response I knew I would get.

"Sometimes people I know will let me stay with them. Some have apartments. That's always nice. Mostly I bounce from here to there. There's a shelter I stay at once in a while. Good people there. But I don't like to take a spot from somebody who needs it more than me."

"What about the money you get every month?" I blurted out.

"What about it?"

I was reluctant to press her about it further but found I couldn't keep myself from the truth.

"Why don't you use that money for rent?"

Her hand twitched involuntarily against the table. "That money doesn't go very far, Charlie. I usually spend it right away on stuff I shouldn't. I know it's stupid, but I don't know any other way. This life is just who I am."

I considered her admission. My mother was a college-educated drug addict from an affluent family living on the streets because the simple fact was she was never anyone's priority. I couldn't stand the thought of continuing the cycle.

Before finishing her burger, she excused herself to go to the restroom. I had a feeling she didn't actually have any need for the facilities, but instead felt she couldn't make it through the meal without taking another hit of whatever she was on. In her absence, I hastily pulled a pen from my knapsack and began writing her a note on a paper napkin.

> Mom,
>
> I want you to know I don't blame you for what happened in your life and I know you did the best you could. Under different circumstances, you would have been the most amazing mother.
>
> Your parents and my father let you down, but not because of anything you did. It was because they were cowards, too afraid of disappointing strangers to honor their relationship with you. I promise you that if I ever become a dad, I will love my kids the way you were never loved. Unconditionally.
>
> I won't be able to see you again after today, and I wanted you to know it isn't your fault. I made a promise that must be kept, and my future depends on maintaining that trust. Please know that if it was within my power to cure you of your addictions, I would. But I think now that's up to you.
>
> With love from your son,
> Charlie

I tucked the napkin under my leg as she returned to the booth, her eyes glazed and bloodshot. She finished her meal without attempting any further conversation.

"You want an apple pie? Maybe for the road?" I asked as she slurped the last of her soda through her straw.

"Yeah," she said. "I'd like that."

I handed her five dollars. "Go pick out what you want. I'll wait here."

While she waited at the counter, I carefully folded the napkin and placed it into the duffle she left sitting on the bench. She returned with vanilla soft serve for both of us and a small stack of apple pies she tossed into her bag.

"I really need to thank you," she said.

"For what?"

"For the food. And for caring enough to come and find me once you found out the truth about your adoption." She licked her cone. "Why *did* you come find me?"

Her question caught me off guard. In all the days I'd been searching, I still hadn't pinpointed what was so important about finding her. I wanted to hear the truth, of course, but somewhere along the way, my search for her had become about more than that. It had become about finding myself.

"I guess I just wanted to hear your story. I wanted to find out where I came from. Who I came from."

"I'm sorry all you found was me."

I locked eyes with her, and for an instant, caught a glimpse of the girl she'd once been. And then, it was quickly overshadowed by the presence of her own self-loathing. She truly believed she was unworthy of love. And not only love from others, but love from herself as well. It was the conviction on which she based all her life's decisions.

"Why would you say that?" I asked.

She finished the last bite of her cone and licked her fingers unapologetically. "Because it's true. You came looking for someone to fill a role in your life. A role I'm not cut out for. I'm never gonna be anybody's mom, Charlie."

"That's not true," I replied. "I don't need you to be my mom.

When you gave me up, you made sure I had a mom. A mom that could do the things you weren't able to do at that time, through no fault of your own. And so what I need isn't another mother. What I need is simply this… for you to know that you are loved. Not because of what you did or didn't do for the past 20 years, but just because you are someone special. You are Victoria Weddington, and you gave birth to a baby boy who loves you, no strings attached."

Tears pooled in her eyes. "I don't like to talk about this stuff. It hurts too much. I don't wanna think about it."

"Okay. We don't have to talk about it. But you deserve good things, Mom. You deserve to be loved."

She fidgeted with her hands in her lap, refusing to look at me again. "I think I should get going now," she said, sliding out of the booth.

"Can I drive you somewhere? Somewhere safe?" I followed her across the dining room to the door.

"Nah. I'll be fine. Lasted this long without a knight in shining armor." She glanced up at me. "I'm glad you came. It's nice, knowing you turned out to be such a great kid. You would've been a mess if you'd stayed with me. Your father knew it the minute he saw us. He knew I'd ruin your life and he was right." She reached up to touch my cheek. "But look at you now. He must be so proud."

I opened my mouth to tell her the truth. I started to explain how I disappointed my father at every turn growing up, and that I was an abysmal failure in his eyes. But when I looked at her, I realized she didn't need to hear the truth. No good could come of knowing she gave me up to a man who barely tolerated me. I couldn't do it. I wouldn't.

"He is," I replied instead.

"I am too," she said.

With that, she opened the door and disappeared into the glare of the afternoon sun. I wanted desperately to go after her, but I was frozen in place by her final declaration. With those words, she became to me the most unlikely of benefactors, presenting me with a gift I didn't realize I needed until after it was given.

My mother was proud of me.

The entire drive back home, I wavered between anger and despair. There seemed no end to the pool of hatred I felt for my father. It was trumped only by the anguish I felt knowing my mother's death was imminent and that I would never see her again.

Two days later, I locked my bathroom door behind me and settled myself on the floor. I watched the hands of my watch counting the minutes until the transfer would occur, returning me to the present timeline. My stomach churned as I considered the consequences of the changes I made, and as a bright flash blinded my vision, I silently prayed I would find my world just as I left it.

PART THREE

CHAPTER TWENTY TWO

Upon my return to the time travel facility, it took several seconds for my eyes to adjust to the dim chamber. Once I regained my sight, I noticed two agents standing in the adjacent room through the window. It seemed odd that they would send more than one person to take me home, but the relief of being back overshadowed the strangeness of their presence. The door slid open with a faint hiss. Both men turned to face me as I stepped into the room.

"Mr. Johnson, we're with the Department of Travel and we're here to detain you for questioning and place you under arrest. Your trip was in violation of time travel code, section 17, article 2."

I stopped breathing as my mind went blank. Something was terribly wrong. My legs buckled beneath me, and I struggled to remain upright, steadying myself on the metal doorframe. I tried to speak, but there was no air in my lungs. I took a deep breath, and with considerable effort, found my voice. "I have no idea what that is. I don't know what happened. What did I do?"

The closest agent reached out to take my arm. His grip was firm and his fingers dug into my flesh. "You need to come with us. Your case worker will be able to explain the charges once you're processed."

Oh God, I thought. *What about Brooke? I promised I'd come for her.*

"A phone! Please, I need to make a phone call!"

"You'll be allowed one call from downstairs."

My head was spinning, and I leaned against the agent as we made our way out of the chamber and into the hallway. As I was led through a series of narrow corridors and staircases, each one looking exactly like the last, I struggled to make sense of what was happening. I tried desperately to recall a single event during my trip which would have resulted in my arrest. By the time we reached In-Processing, I had all but given up on trying to figure out what I'd done wrong. I assumed I was about to find out.

They delivered me to an area which reminded me of every interrogation room I'd seen on TV. There were no windows and the only light came from a single incandescent fixture on the ceiling. I was instructed to sit at the table in the center of the room and without any further explanation, both men disappeared out the door, which closed with a resounding thud behind them. Panic overtook me. Then I remembered my phone call.

"Hello!" I cried out. "I'd like to make my phone call please! Hello?"

There was no immediate response and was about to call out again when the door creaked open. An unfamiliar officer placed a phone on the table and stationed himself stoically beside the door.

"You may make one call. Please be advised that your conversation is being recorded."

I reached for the phone, and without stopping to consider other options, immediately dialed Brooke's number. It rang once. Twice. Three times. Then it clicked to voicemail. I ended the call and tried again, frantically pressing the redial button. This time, instead of ringing, it went directly to her recorded message. I closed my eyes and listened to her voice. As I was about to leave a message, I reconsidered, remembering that she was supposed to have been waiting for me at my house. I hung up a second time and entered my family's phone number onto the keypad. I held my breath as the call connected.

"Johnson residence."

It wasn't my mom who answered the phone. It wasn't Melody either.

"Dad?" I whispered.

"Charlie? Is that you? Speak up, Son. I can barely hear you," my father snapped.

For a second, his voice didn't register in my head. It was as if I stepped inside a movie, and my life was not my own.

But it was my life. And my father was still in it. The phone dropped from my hand onto the table.

The reason for my arrest became painfully clear.

I steadied my hand to retrieve the phone from the table.

"It's me," I confirmed.

"Where the hell are you? Why are you calling from a government exchange?"

"I'm here, Dad."

"Where's here? Tell me what's going on this instant!"

I tried to clear my head. I knew my father's presence was the direct result of whatever law I'd broken, and there was no avoiding the punishment I was about to face.

"I'm at a time travel facility, about 30 minutes east." I paused, gathering the strength to say what needed to be said. "I used my trip, Dad," I told him bluntly. "I found out about the secret you've been keeping from me my entire life. If you'd have told me the truth on your own, maybe I wouldn't have done what I did. But what's done is done."

"The truth about what? What are you rambling about?"

"The truth about my adoption. About my mother. About what you did to her." I felt my courage growing. "I know everything."

I could hear his shallow breathing, and pictured him regaining his composure on the other end of the line. He coughed into the receiver.

"Just come home, Charlie, so we can discuss this in private."

"I *can't* come home. That's why I'm calling."

"Why *can't* you come home?" he asked, unable to mask his annoyance.

"I've been arrested. Apparently I broke one of the traveling laws during my trip. I think I know now what I did, but I have no idea how I did it. I'm probably going to need an attorney so you're going to need to get me one," I said, surprising myself with my boldness. "Send him here to the facility."

"What am I supposed to tell him?"

"I don't know! But I'm going to need as much help as I can get." My mind raced. I felt like I was forgetting something important. Suddenly, I remembered Brooke. "Has anyone talked to Brooke today? Is she there at the house?"

"No. I didn't know to expect her."

My heart sank. "Well, she should be on her way, so when she gets to the house, send her to the facility as well."

"Charlie, I don't understand what's happened. What have you done?"

"I don't know exactly. But unlike you, I'm going to take responsibility for my actions."

"What's that supposed to mean?" he yelled.

"Just get me a lawyer!" I ordered as I clicked the button, ending the call.

I was offered a bottled water by a petite woman in a pantsuit three sizes too large for her tiny frame. I declined the beverage, and she sat across from me at the table.

"Hello, Charles," she said.

"Good morning," I replied.

"My name is Leigh Cavanaugh. I handle new cases here at this facility. I've been informed that you are waiting for an attorney to be present before we speak?"

"Yes."

"I believe I just saw someone arrive for you. He should be here any minute."

There was an uncomfortable silence between us as the minutes ticked by. Finally the metal door from the hallway creaked open, and a formidable looking man stepped into the room.

"Charles Johnson?" he asked.

"That's me."

He extended his hand as he sat in the chair beside me. "I'm Patrick Miller. I've known your dad for a long time. Let's find out what's going on here."

"Are you ready to begin?" Ms. Cavanaugh asked.

I nodded.

She cleared her throat dramatically. "Please be advised that we are being recorded and that anything you say or do can be used against you during the hearing process. My name is Leigh Cavanaugh. I am with Mr. Charles Johnson, the accused, and his attorney, Mr. Patrick Miller is also present. Mr. Johnson, we have tangible evidence of you making changes to the past during government sanctioned trip 396DIB92 resulting in a life or lives being saved. This is a violation of time travel code, section 17, article 2. You do understand that the contract you signed prior to your departure defined the terms of your passage through time, and clearly stated that it is against the law to make any changes to your timeline?"

My head was spinning. "Yes," I replied.

"I am obligated to inform you, the penalty for saving a life during a trip can be up to 15 years in prison with a minimum sentence of 10 years. It is one of the most highly penalized offenses and you should know that accused parties are rarely released on technicalities. You will be given an opportunity to make a statement to the overseeing board, but given the solid evidence against you, I cannot allow you to leave this facility until after the board has heard your case."

"No bond?" asked Miller.

"Not for this offense."

"How long until the hearing?" Miller continued.

"It usually happens pretty quickly. Three days? Five at the max. Mr. Johnson will be given accommodations here at the facility until that time."

The grimness of my situation uncoiled like a cobra warming in the sun. My father's presence was the only proof the government needed to convict me. There was no question I would spend the next decade in prison. And while I was rotting away behind metal bars, the future I imagined for myself would disappear like Brigadoon in the fog.

In that moment I understood, I was never going to marry Brooke.

The thought of her brought a stabbing pain to my chest. My Brooke. My smart, sweet Brooke. She had warned me repeatedly about the serious nature of time travel. Of the inevitable chances I was taking with our future. I suddenly regretted not taking her advice more seriously. I needed to see her. I needed to see her right away.

"What about visitors," I asked.

Ms. Cavanaugh seemed startled by the question. "Uh, yes, you will be allowed visitors."

"When?"

"Once we've finished here, you'll complete your processing and be taken to your quarters. You should be allowed visitors after that time."

"Are we finished then?"

She gazed curiously across the table at me. "I suppose we could be. For now. I assumed you or your attorney would have some questions."

Miller pushed his chair back from the table, scraping the metal feet against the linoleum floor. "Perhaps we will have some questions later, after Mr. Johnson has had the opportunity to assess his situation."

Ms. Cavanaugh gathered her papers, and stood up. "Please feel free to contact me. In the meantime, if you would like some time alone together to discuss your case, you are welcome to stay here. If not, I can take you straight to processing."

Without a moment's hesitation, I headed for the door.

"Mr. Johnson, don't you think it would be wise for us to discuss this matter further?" Miller asked as I reached the threshold.

The only thing I cared about in that moment was finding the shortest route to Brooke. I knew I wouldn't be able to concentrate on getting myself out of the mess I created until after I was given a opportunity to see her.

"Any chance you'd be willing to come back tonight? I really need some time to wrap my head around what's going on. Maybe you could look into my options, and we can talk about them after dinner?"

He glanced at his watch and picked up his computer bag. "Sure. I can be back at seven. It's a pleasure to meet you, Charlie. I'm just sorry it's under these circumstances."

"Me too," I replied, shaking his hand.

I followed him down the hall, until he turned left in the direction of the exit. Ms. Cavanaugh headed right, hurrying me through a series of narrow hallways until we reached a hectic office at the far end of the facility. An older gentleman, wearing a seersucker suit and reading spectacles, was being escorted through the doorway as we entered. His presence did little to curb my growing apprehension.

"This way," Ms. Cavanaugh called over her shoulder, as we approached several rows of chairs, reminiscent of unpleasant trips to the Department of Motor Vehicles.

"Have a seat here. Your name is already in the queue so when a booking officer calls for you, I'll take you over to his window. Once you're finished being processed, another officer will take you to your assigned location."

"What about visitors?"

"After you're finished."

"How long will it take to be finished?"

She scanned the room of waiting detainees. "An hour. Maybe more."

"Maybe less?" I offered hopefully.

She suppressed a smile. "Doubtful. I admire your enthusiasm though." She scrolled through a file on her tablet. "I have a couple others to check in on. I'll be back when I hear your name called."

"Thanks," I replied thinly.

After watching her approach a haggard looking businessman, I scanned my fellow offenders seated around the room. I was struck immediately by the severe lack of diversity among the group. Most were men. Middle aged. Caucasian. Their clothing suggested affluence. I wondered what would account for the lack of women. Or elderly. Or impoverished. Regardless of the composition of the group, it was evident there was no shortage of people breaking the traveling laws. I never considered how many violators there actually were in the world. I couldn't help but wonder just how much of my life was affected by time travel. Judging by the lack of open seating in the room, it was probably more than I had ever imagined.

I thought about Brooke and the changes she made during her trips to the past. It dawned on me that she had never been arrested, even though she admitted a life was lost as a direct result of the changes she made during her second trip. Would taking a life not be more of an offense than saving one? I was disturbed by the obvious inconsistencies in the agency's accountability standards and arrest methods. Clearly I was missing something.

Dozens of names were announced over the intercom. I watched as one after another, the men around me were escorted to the glass windows. While I waited my turn, I reflected upon my father's return to my life. From the second I heard his voice on the phone, I couldn't deny my feelings of disappointment. As I sat picking at the ripped corner of the vinyl chair, facing imprisonment as a result of his presence, the disappointment I felt quickly turned to resentment.

His life had been spared. Mine was being taken away.

"Charles Johnson," the intercom announced.

It took several seconds to register that my name was being called. Ms. Cavanaugh appeared out of nowhere and walked me to the counter where a uniformed officer waited. She wore a look of indifference and a severe looking hair style.

"Identification?"

I handed her my card. She swiped it across the computer screen.

"Charles Johnson, you have been accused of breaking the time travel code, section 17, article 2 during trip 396DIB92. You will have a hearing to discuss your case later in the week. Until that time, you are required to remain here at the facility. After your hearing, if you are found not guilty, you will be free to go. If you are found guilty, you will receive your sentencing immediately and will be transferred to our long term housing facility. I understand you have chosen to have an attorney present at your proceedings?"

"Yes."

"Fine. Then I think we are done here. Do you have any questions?"

"Long term housing facility? Isn't that just another name for jail?"

She glared at me over the top of her glasses. "We prefer long term housing facility. It's reserved only for violators of traveling laws. Any other questions?"

I thought of Brooke. "When can I see visitors?"

"You may make a formal request to the floor supervisor when you arrive. Officer Gordon will escort you there now. Have a good day, Mr. Johnson."

I was taken aback by her lack of compassion. "I didn't mean to change anything. It was an accident," I said.

"Yeah. You and everybody else around here. Have a good day."

I ignored her sentiments, said goodbye to Ms. Cavanaugh, and begrudgingly followed Officer Gordon back out the way I came. We stopped at the elevator adjacent to the main entrance to take us below ground to the holding cells. As we waited for the doors to open, I craned my neck in an attempt to see into the front lobby.

She was there. Her hands were folded in her lap, and her face was streaked with tears. She stared straight ahead at the wall, engrossed in her own thoughts. I called to her.

Her reaction was immediate. She rose from her seat in one fluid motion, turning in the direction of my voice. She began running toward me, pushing past everyone who stood between us.

"Where are you going?" she cried.

"Downstairs. I have to stay for now. Wait for me. They said I can see you soon."

The doors to the elevator slid open and the officer directed me inside.

"I'll wait for you," I heard Brooke call as the doors shut, blocking her from my view.

As the elevator descended into the depths of the facility, I shuddered, wondering how many years she would be willing to wait.

CHAPTER TWENTY THREE

After over an hour of processing, which included taking my statement as well as a lot of other useless personal information, my name finally made its way to the top of the visitor's waiting list, and I was escorted to the visitation area on the main floor of the building. I sat alone, rubbing my temples at one of the six plastic picnic tables in the room, willing myself to wake up from the nightmare my life had become. I glanced around, half expecting a TV personality to breeze in and announce the location of the hidden cameras. We'd all share a good laugh, and I'd go home.

The joke was on me. No celebrities arrived.

Instead, three additional travelers sat at separate tables around the room. Behind me, there was a frazzled, middle-aged man shouting obscenities at a woman in a crisp, linen pantsuit. I hoped for her sake she was his lawyer, not his wife. An older gentleman embraced a considerably younger woman at the only table beside the window. She repeatedly cried out, as though her grief was causing her physical distress, each time startling me from my thoughts. My final companion sat alone, as I did, elbows on the table, cradling his head in his hands.

After several minutes, a buzzer sounded and I watched in anguish as the guard hoisted himself from his chair and shuffled to the metal gate.

"Visitor for Charles Johnson," he announced. "Thirty minutes begins now."

I stood up as she crossed the length of the room, her footsteps echoing off the concrete floor. I had never seen her so haggard, with her hair piled haphazardly on top of her head and her eyes wild with despair. It was like a knife to my heart, knowing I was the reason for her grief. I folded her into my chest where she began to sob uncontrollably.

"Oh, Charlie! I can't believe they came for you!"

I led her to the table, and we sat wrapped in one another's arms, each supporting the weight of the other.

"My father's still alive," I said, after she calmed down.

"Yes. The accident never happened. He never fell into the ravine. You and I thought for sure they'd have come for you already, if they were going to. I guess the government was waiting for you to return to the present timeline."

"What happened on the day he was supposed to have died?"

"We waited for it to happen. We knew it was coming. And then you called me that afternoon to tell me he came home. We were really worried because we couldn't figure out what was happening. At first we were scared because we thought he lived because of something you did, but when the authorities never arrived, we assumed someone else caused the change. I guess we were right to have been worried after all."

I mulled over the new information. "I don't know how to feel about it. I wish I was happy. But given the circumstances…"

"I know. But to be honest, you haven't known how to feel about it since it happened. Or didn't happen." She shook her head in disbelief. "We thought the authorities would show up right away, but then they didn't and we were so relieved. We knew the entire timeline was going to change after that, so we tried to keep things the same as they were the first time around. It was really hard though, considering everything was completely different." She paused to look at my face, brushing the hair off my forehead. "I headed to your house this morning, just like we planned for me to do after your extraction from the past. Your family was freaking out. They told me about your phone call, and I came straight here. I've been waiting in the lobby ever since. Your mom and dad and Melody got here about half an hour ago. They're second on your list of visitors."

As excited as I was about seeing my mom and Melody, I couldn't stand the thought of being in my father's presence. Knowing how he treated my mother, I still couldn't stand the thought of being in the same room with him. And yet, I was indebted to him. The lawyer he supplied provided my only chance of avoiding prison.

"What am I going to do, Brooke?" I asked, resting my chin on the top of her head.

"I don't know. What did they tell you? Are there any loopholes? Is there any way out of it?"

I shook my head. "No. It sounds like a pretty cut and dried case. My father is probably the only evidence they need. The lawyer said he would try to figure something out. Maybe the fact I didn't do it on purpose will count for something. Who knows?"

"How long do we have until the hearing?"

"A couple of days."

"And if the lawyer doesn't come up with anything?"

I didn't answer. I couldn't.

She prodded. "What's gonna happen, Charlie? Tell me."

"Prison. Ten to fifteen years."

It is possible to see a person's spirit drain from her body, because that's what I saw happen to Brooke. One second, she was there. The next second, she was gone.

I wanted to tell her that everything was going to be okay. That we would get through it. That it would make us stronger. Better.

But I couldn't lie to her.

"I don't expect you to wait for me. I don't even want you to. You should go back to school. Find someone else. Enjoy a wonderful life. It's what you deserve."

She didn't blink, sitting motionless beside me, in a daze, as our allotted visitation ticked away. Finally, she tilted her head ever so slightly to gaze up at me. A tiny smile pulled at the corner of her mouth.

"I was going to say yes today. Yes to your marriage proposal. I've been holding off saying anything because I told you I was going to make you wait until you got back. It's been hard, keeping my answer from you all this time. When I woke up this morning, the excitement of telling you nearly overwhelmed me."

"We don't have to talk about it, Brooke. Please don't torture yourself."

She stared at her hands, picking at a cuticle which began to bleed. "It's a long time, isn't it? Fifteen years?"

"Yes. A very long time."

"Is there any hope at all?"

I knew there wasn't. I wasted our second chance. But I didn't have the courage to say it aloud.

"There's always hope," I replied, taking her hands in mine.

Tears pooled in her eyes. "I have faith," she said. "Faith that I wouldn't have been led to you if I wasn't meant to be with you always. Somehow we'll be together."

There were a thousand reasons to love Brooke. As I sat holding her, straddling the plastic picnic table bench, I added another reason to the list. She was tenacious. As exasperating as it was inspiring, I had never witnessed anyone so confident in her life's path. I'd never known her to question why things happened. She just accepted and worked with the hand she was dealt the best she knew how. I guess that wisdom came from trying to save Branson. The experience had obviously taught her a lot. I wondered what wisdom I would gain from my experience.

I couldn't look at her any longer. "But if it doesn't work out…"

"Something will work out. It might not be what we want. It might not be what we're expecting. But something will work out."

The overhead speaker crackled to life. "Charles Johnson, time is up. Your guest needs to leave the visitation area," the guard announced.

Her face was only inches from mine. I could smell her cherry lip balm. I breathed it in deeply, hoping to capture the memory and carry it with me into the night.

"Don't go," I said, brushing my cheek against her forehead.

"You heard him. I have to leave. Your family wants to see you too." She kissed me. Passionately. I felt the longing pass between us. "I'll come back tomorrow. First thing."

She stood up and hurried to the door. I knew she wouldn't dawdle. Quick goodbyes, she said, were less painful.

She glanced over her shoulder as she passed through the metal gate. She mouthed the words, "I love you."

"I love you, too," I replied.

Less than five minutes later, Melody appeared at the gate, waving frantically alongside my parents. After being admitted, she raced between the tables and nearly tackled me with her embrace.

"Charlie, when are they letting you go?" she asked.

"Don't know, kiddo. I guess we'll find out in a couple of days."

"What'd you do?"

"He used his stupid trip, that's what he did!" my father bellowed as he strode across the room. "And royally screwed everything up, just like always."

"That's not fair, Phil," Mom chimed in, kissing me on the cheek. "You should at least give him a chance to explain what happened."

Without so much as a hug or a handshake, he sat down and folded his hands on the table. "Yes. I'd like nothing more than to hear how exactly you got yourself into this mess. And there had better be a reasonable explanation."

I sat down across the table from my father. Melody slid in beside me, and Mom took the remaining seat next to my father. "Whatever I did was an accident," I said.

"Oh, fabulous. An accident. I guess that makes it all better." He sneered at me. "How in the world is it going to look for a United States Senator to have a son in prison? Do you have any idea what this will do to my career if it gets out? You never think about how your actions affect other people, Charlie. You never have."

"That's all I ever do!" I replied. "I've spent my entire life considering how my every move is going to affect your precious political career."

"Obviously this time you didn't!" he countered. "What you've just done could kill my campaign for reelection."

I couldn't help but smile at him. "Kill it, huh? It's funny you should bring up death. I suspect no one's told you why I've been arrested?"

"We keep asking," Mom said, blotting her eyes with a tissue, "but they refuse to tell us anything."

I reached across the table to take her hand. I could not ignore the tormented look on her face and wished there was something I could say to ease her pain. "I'm here because during my trip, I ended up saving someone's life."

"Why would you do that? You know it's against the law!" my father said, cursing under his breath.

"I assure you," I replied, matching the intensity of his stare with my own, "it was an accident."

"Who did you save?" Melody asked.

"I saved him," I said, gesturing toward my father.

"What?" my mother cried. "Phil died?"

"Yeah. In a freak climbing accident. Went on one of his buddy weekend expeditions and ended up dead at the bottom of a ravine."

"I don't believe you," he said.

I laughed. I couldn't help it. He was never going to change.

"You don't have to believe me, *Dad*," I said sharply, spitting his name like poison from my tongue. "There will be a hearing later this week, and you'll get to hear all about how I inadvertently saved your life."

"Then why did you go back, if it wasn't to save Dad's life?" Melody asked.

I turned to my sister. It was obvious she'd been crying as well. I quickly decided to edit the story of what happened to spare her feelings. She didn't need to hear what a horrible man her father was.

At least not right away.

"After he died, I convinced Mom to tell me something they hid from me my entire life. She told me I was adopted. I started looking for my biological mother and found out she died too. There were some answers I needed to get that could only come from her. You had the idea of going back in time to see her so I could find the closure I was looking for. And that's what I did."

Everyone was silent for several moments, allowing the truth of what transpired to sink in fully. My father looked at me skeptically, knowing I intentionally chose to share the abridged story of my adoption. I knew he couldn't fathom why I would spare them the truth. Empathy was lost on him.

Finally, Mom spoke.

"So how did you end up accidentally saving Dad?"

"I have no idea," I replied.

I watched my father, mulling over my revelation. I could see the torment etched in the lines of his face as he attempted to appear unaffected by the news of his own death.

"What's done is done," he said finally. "At least some good came of Charlie's horrible lack of judgment. Now all we can do is leave it up to the court to decide your fate. I'll pull as many strings as I can from my end. Lord knows, I certainly don't need any sort of scandal this close to November elections."

My mother bowed her head as she silently acquiesced to her husband's assessment of the situation.

We were interrupted by the hum of reverberation as the speaker system crackled to life once again. "Charles Johnson, time is up. Your guest needs to leave the visitation area," the guard announced for the second time.

I stood up to acknowledge my family's departure. Melody nestled herself against me in the space beneath my arm and began to cry.

"It's gonna be okay, Mel," I consoled her. "Someone will figure something out. Have faith."

Mom scooted around the table and approached me hesitantly. "I always wanted to tell you the truth about your adoption," she whispered as she reached to embrace me. "I hope you can forgive me."

"You have nothing to be forgiven for," I whispered back, hugging her tightly.

"I love you, Charlie," she said.

"I love you too, Mom," I replied.

I followed my family to the exit. As the metal gate began to close behind them, my father stopped short and turned to face me, grabbing me by the front of my shirt. I thought, for an instant, he was going to apologize as he pulled my face close to his.

"I don't know what that little tramp Victoria told you, but I'm sure she filled your head with venomous lies. I stand by my decision to keep you in the dark about the entire situation, and I expect that you will keep your mouth shut about it, if you know what's good for you."

I pulled away from him. He released his grip on my shirt just before the fibers began to tear. "You're a monster," I said.

"Just keep your mouth shut, Charlie, and maybe I'll see about getting you out of here," he replied.

He slipped through the opening, and the gate latched behind him. As I watched my family making their way to the end of the corridor, I was thankful they came to see me. Especially my father. Speaking with him confirmed any doubts I had regarding many of the decisions I'd made since his death. I knew the insight I gained during my time with Victoria were invaluable, as they allowed me to see my father in a whole new light.

No longer did I fear his disappointment or feel the need to garner his approval. She showed me the truth about his character, and so, it was with disgust that I watched him turn the corner toward the exit, from the building, and also, from my life.

CHAPTER TWENTY FOUR

After a dinner of soggy fish sticks, burnt French fries, and overcooked string beans, I returned to the visitation area to wait for Miller. I clung to the hope he'd found a loophole in the course of the afternoon to procure my freedom. My entire future was riding on his ability to work the system in my favor.

I had never been so uncertain of anything in my life.

When the guard announced his arrival, I couldn't bring myself to stand and greet him. He sauntered across the room, carrying several files in his arms. He tossed them on the table and plopped himself heavily on the bench beside me.

"How's it going, Charlie?"

"Couldn't be better," I replied wryly.

He chuckled. "That good, huh?" he said as he shuffled through his paperwork. "I guess this isn't really a happening kind of place."

He hesitated, as if he was waiting for me to engage him in small talk. When, after several seconds, I didn't respond, he finally continued.

"Well, I guess we should start by discussing what I found out about your case today. Unfortunately, the government only released parts of your file. The full account won't be available until tomorrow, but I can share the little bit I have right now." He paused to put on a pair of reading glasses from his jacket pocket. "As you already know, your father's presence in the current timeline is a direct result of a change made during your trip. The government has proof the change was caused by something you did. Something about a glitch in the timeline monitoring module. I honestly have no idea what that means – I've never even heard of a timeline monitoring module before - but it's what is listed as their evidence. Additionally, there is a second person listed in the report who is currently alive because of your trip. They haven't released the person's name, but I have to be honest, Charlie… It was going to be hard enough convincing them that saving one life was a mistake. Two is going to be nearly impossible."

I stared blankly at the wall. The revelation of having saved a second life was more than I could wrap my head around. I thought about Brooke taking three trips to save one life on purpose. It was ironic that I saved two without even trying. What were the chances?

"Look, legally, there's not really much I can do to help you. They have evidence you saved both lives from their timeline monitoring module. They know you broke the law. We know your father was one of the people you saved. It's going to be hard to convince them you didn't save him on purpose."

I glared at him. I wanted to share my true feelings about my father, but I knew it wouldn't help. Neither he nor the panel would believe me.

"I didn't save anyone on purpose."

"I get it. You didn't mean to, but you did anyway. And there's not much I can do about it now. The best we can do is to beg the board for leniency and hope for the best. There are no loopholes, Charlie. I'm sorry."

"Not as sorry as I am," I said.

He shook his head and gathered his papers. "For what it's worth, I'm sure there are a lot of people who would be grateful to know you saved Phil's life. The world needs as many men like your dad as it can get."

There was no shortage of people my father sufficiently duped into believing he was the perfect man. Perfect husband. Perfect father. Perfect civic leader. I was sure at that very moment my father was spinning the story of my imprisonment in a way that would show him in the best possible light. A son saving his father's life would be a captivating human interest story. By morning, he would have every major television network on the phone to discuss how I selflessly used my trip to save his life. Because my love for him was so strong, even the threat of prison didn't stop me.

When I didn't respond, Miller stood up from the table and placed his hand on my shoulder. "If I come across something to help, I'll be in touch. Otherwise, I'll be back just before the hearing. It's scheduled for Friday morning at 11AM. We can review your testimony and make sure we have our ducks in a row, so to speak. Anyway, have a good night, Charlie."

He saw himself to the exit. A guard escorted me to my assigned cell, where I proceeded to have the worst night of my life. I fluctuated between hopefulness and despair as I tossed and turned on the tiny mattress late into the night. Staring at a lengthy crack in the ceiling, I tried to convince myself all was not lost. Surely, upon hearing my testimony, the board would simply throw out my case and allow me to return to my life. I wasn't a criminal. I hadn't intended on breaking any rules. At least not that particular rule.

As the hours dragged on, I remembered the articles I read as a child, documenting the government's strict enforcement policies. I knew they wouldn't be concerned with my intentions. They only cared that I broke the law. The government wouldn't miss the opportunity to make me an example for other would-be travelers.

Morning found me despondent and anxious. I knew Brooke would return at some point before lunch. The thought of seeing her was my greatest joy and also my greatest sadness, for I knew deep down that our relationship was about to end. Our days together were numbered.

By the time the guard announced her arrival, it was midmorning. Depression cloaked me in its suffocating embrace.

"You look awful," she said as she wrapped her arms around my neck.

"Thanks," I replied, holding her tightly. "I probably feel worse than I look."

We stood, holding one another, her head resting on my chest. I closed my eyes, absorbing her warmth and strength. I didn't want to forget how amazing it felt to press my body against hers because I knew in the coming years, the memory of her embrace would be all I'd have to hold onto.

She pulled away, returning me to reality. My arms fell to my sides as she sat at the table.

"What did the lawyer say? Can he get you out?"

There was a strong possibility we would never be together outside prison walls again. I was hesitant to speak the words aloud, but I wouldn't sugar coat the truth. I owed her that much.

"No. I don't think so."

Anger flashed across her face. "Why not?"

"Because it would have been hard enough if I had only saved my father. But apparently, there's someone else as well."

"Someone else? Who?"

"I don't know for sure. But I have an idea."

She rested her head in her hands, unwilling to look me in the eye. I reached out to caress her cheek, but she recoiled at my touch.

"Two lives, Charlie? Two!" she snapped. "How could you be so careless? How could you?"

"I'm sorry. I…"

"I'm sorry isn't enough, Charlie! You were supposed to be *my* life! You were supposed to be my *husband*. I should have never agreed to any of this. I should have talked you out of using your trip!"

"I know. You were right. I'm so sorry."

We sat together in silence, side by side on the picnic table bench for several minutes. She didn't move, but I could tell her mind was racing.

"Your mother is the other one," she said finally.

"Probably."

"Do you want me to find out?"

"Miller said the file would be released sometime today. Then we'll know for sure. My hearing is set for Friday."

I followed her gaze out the window at two robins sitting on the ledge.

"Do you want me to go find her? To see what happened?" she asked.

She was looking at me again. Looking at me with the same compassion I'd seen on her face when she treated a wounded animal. Or studied with a struggling classmate. Or helped a friend mend a broken heart. I wasn't worthy of her compassion, and yet here she was, giving it freely.

"Really?"

"Yes, really. If she's still alive, then something you said or did kept her from dying. Do you want me to go find out what happened?"

"Why would you do that?"

She shrugged her shoulders. "Your mother is the reason for all of this. You wanted to know her truth. Maybe knowing what happened might help get you out of here." She turned from me again, throwing her hands up in frustration. "What do I know? It's the only thing I can think of, and I can't just sit here doing nothing. I want to help."

And there it was. A funny thing about life is, regardless of the situation, you always are who you are. And regardless of the situation, Brooke Wallace was always a doer. She never sat on the sidelines. She always got involved.

"You're one special girl, you know that?"

She blushed involuntarily, making a face.

"It's a long drive. I hate the thought of you going alone."

"Stop being overprotective," she replied. "I'll take Melody. We can leave this afternoon."

"When will you be back?"

"I'll make sure we're back before your hearing, regardless of whether we're able to find her."

I smiled at her. I didn't believe that anything she might find in South Carolina would help me avoid imprisonment, but I wasn't going to stop her from trying to help. She slid across the bench, draped her legs over mine, and rested her head on my shoulder.

185

"I wish time travel had never been invented," she said.

"Me too. But then again, if it had never been invented, you never would've tried to save your brother. Instead of going to college, you might still be at home, suffering from depression. And if you never went to college, you wouldn't have met me." I paused. "So it can't be all bad, right?"

"No. It can't be all bad," she agreed. "I wouldn't trade our love to avoid the pain we're about to endure."

"Hey. Don't be so pessimistic. Maybe it will all work out," I said in a voice that betrayed my true feelings.

"And maybe pigs will fly," she sighed.

We held one another until the guard announced our time was up. As she slid from my arms, it dawned on me that I might never hold her again. I panicked.

"Don't leave me," I whispered, grabbing for her arm as she walked away.

"I have to go, Charlie. I don't want to get you in trouble."

"No," I said, pulling her close once again, "I can't stand the thought of losing you. Of you not being a part of my life."

She stood on her tiptoes and draped her arms around my neck. "No matter what happens, I will always be a part of your life. I love you. Nothing is going to change that. Ever."

"I'm not going to hold you to that," I said.

"You won't have to."

She kissed me. Her lips were familiar. Soft. Warm. They reminded me of just how much I stood to lose.

"I have to go."

"I know. Please be safe out there. Especially on the drive south."

"I will. And stop sounding like my dad." She smiled. "See you when I get back."

"Okay." She made it to the gate before I called to her. "If you see her, my mother... tell her I love her."

"Don't worry. I will."

CHAPTER TWENTY FIVE

Aside from the brief visits with my mom each morning, I spent the next three days alone in my cell. The minutes dragged like hours. The hours felt like days. And I devoted each second to berating myself for every poor decision I made leading to my arrest. I worried endlessly over Brooke and Melody, hating that I had no means of communicating with them.

Mercifully, a guard arrived just after lunch on Thursday to announce there were two visitors waiting for me in the lobby. Instead of feeling elated as I expected, I was overcome by a wave of nausea, unable to stand for several moments. Only when the guard threatened to send them away, did I find the strength to leave my cell.

Brooke and Melody were waiting for me in the visitation area. From the doorway, I watched them huddled together like two schoolgirls with a secret. It was reassuring to know in my absence, they would continue to have each other, but I wondered how long their friendship would last when I was no longer a part of their lives. Would they become yet another casualty of my poor decisions?

Brooke must have felt me watching them. She looked up from their conversation, and as soon as she saw me, her shoulders relaxed. I saw relief wash over her.

The feeling was mutual.

After a quick round of hugs, they sat across the table from me, and I demanded to be filled in on every detail of their trip.

"She's alive, Charlie," Brooke began. "We lucked out with it being the first of the month, so Melody and I waited in the same parking lot by the bank for her to show up. It was getting late in the day, and we were about to give up, but then Melody spotted her coming around the corner."

"She looks exactly like you, Charlie. Only she's old. And a girl. So I guess she only really looks sort of like you," Melody explained.

"Well, I guess I should be glad I don't look like a girl," I laughed, rolling my eyes.

"You'd make a horrible girl," she teased. "Especially with your big, hairy toes!"

Brooke sighed heavily but couldn't contain a smile. "Stop goofing off you two! We only have 30 minutes, and there's a lot to tell."

"We'll be on our best behavior, Drill Sergeant," I said, saluting her. I couldn't deny how much better I felt since they arrived. Love was undeniably therapeutic.

Brooke continued. "By the time we ran across the street, she had already finished at the ATM and was headed back the way she came. We followed her for a few blocks, keeping just out of sight, to see where she was going."

"That was dangerous," I said, interrupting. "She's a drug addict, for crying out loud. Who knows what kind of place she might have led you."

"Just let me tell the story!"

I acquiesced. "Fine. Tell the story."

"She led us to this beautiful four story brick building. Looked like it might have been a municipal office at some point. Anyway, nowadays it's a halfway house."

"Get out!"

"Yeah. She's clean and sober. Been that way since you went to see her last year."

I couldn't believe what she was saying but I needed desperately to hear the rest. "Tell me everything," I said.

She took a deep breath. "So after she went inside, we decided to knock on the door. Somebody else answered it. Some old guy. But he let us in and called for Victoria. Of course she had no idea who we were, but as soon as I explained we were there on your behalf, she opened right up. Apparently whatever you said last year put her on the straight and narrow. She said the day after you left, she called a friend who took her to a narcotics anonymous meeting. She started going every day. They put her in touch with the halfway house where they let her stay as long as she tests clean every week. She got a job cleaning houses through another one of the NA members, and she seems to be doing well. She was happy. And grounded. I think she was a lot different than when you saw her during your trip."

A lump formed in my throat. My mother was alive because of me. It was hard to imagine having such a powerful influence on someone I barely knew. And yet, she told Brooke I was the catalyst for her sobriety. My heart swelled with joy for my mother and the promise of her new life.

"It feels good, huh?" Brooke asked, grinning at me from across the table.

"No. Yes." I fumbled for the right words to explain how I was feeling. "I wasn't trying to solve her problems. I didn't mean to change her life. I just wanted to find out where I came from." I reflected on the broken woman I met on my trip. "I guess it's nice to know that something good came out of all this mess. Who would have thought meeting me would be all it took to save her?"

"You're her kid, Charlie," Melody said. "Maybe she just needed to know somebody loved her."

"Well, let's hope she does something good with her second chance. If you have to spend the next fifteen years behind bars, it's really the least she can do," said Brooke.

"Did you tell her? About me? About the trip?"

"I had to. She mentioned something about a note you gave her saying you couldn't visit her again. She assumed she'd just never hear from you again and was surprised you sent us to see her. I didn't want to make her feel bad about you not coming, so I told her the truth. I didn't know what else to do."

"So she knows that she died in the original timeline?"

"Yes."

"And she knows I'm in prison because I saved her."

"Yeah."

"And what did she say?"

"She cried."

"Happy cried or sad cried?"

She shrugged her shoulders. "Probably both."

I hated the thought of causing my mother pain. I glanced at the clock. We had only eleven minutes left together.

"You haven't told him the best part," said Melody enthusiastically.

Brooke suddenly brightened, her voice raising an octave. "I don't know if it will help, but she said she would come testify on your behalf. She was insistent about it. She wants to make sure they know you didn't tell her about her death or how she died."

I had also considered the possibility of asking for her testimony, but assumed it would be inadmissible given her history of drug abuse. However, if she was no longer using, perhaps the board would allow her to speak.

"I never met my mother in the original timeline," I said. "I wonder if the fact that I went to see her will be considered 'willful intent.'"

"You're already in the worst sort of trouble, Charlie. I don't think letting her testify will do any more harm."

She was right. I didn't really have much to lose. Maybe allowing her to speak would prove to the board it was all a mistake. She could simply tell them I never shared any information about her death or how she died, thereby giving her a means to avoid it. If my father agreed to testify to the same thing, perhaps there was still hope after all.

I smiled at her, reaching for her hands across the table. "Thank you for going to find her."

"You're welcome," she replied, entwining her fingers with mine. "She and I already discussed how to get her here. When visitation is over, I'll head to the bank and wire her money for a bus ticket. She can be here by morning."

She yawned, stretching her arms above her head. Exhaustion colored dark circles under her eyes and her hair was a tousled mess, still piled like a rat's nest on the top of her head. Although she wore no makeup and appeared to have slept in her clothes, I couldn't keep myself from staring at her.

"You may have just saved me. You know that, right?"

"What do you mean?"

"I mean, I had nothing. Not a single defense. My lawyer's barely shown an interest and yet, here you are, providing legitimate testimony and saving the day."

She tucked her hair behind her ears and gazed across the room. "You would have done the same thing for me."

She was right. There was nothing I wouldn't do for her. When you love someone, you do whatever it takes to help them. Protect them. Ensure they remain a part of your life. The fact that she felt that depth of love for me only heightened my desire to be set free.

"So tomorrow's the big day then," I said finally. "I'll either go home with you or be dragged off to prison."

"I don't want to talk about it. Can we just sit here together for the few minutes we have left and not think about how much everything sucks?"

"Yes. We can do that."

I joined them on their side of the table and wrapped my arms around their shoulders, holding them close. When our time together ended, I walked them to the gate, where it was impossible to remain stoic as they both kissed me tearfully goodbye.

"We'll see you in the morning," Brooke promised.

"I'm crossing all my fingers and my toes," added Melody.

I couldn't keep myself from grinning at her. Her youthful optimism was infectious. "I love you both. No matter what happens tomorrow, I'll never stop."

I watched them walk all the way down the hall until they turned the corner toward the exit. Just before she disappeared out of sight, Brooke turned to me with a tearful smile and tiny wave. It broke my heart. In less than 24 hours I would know my fate. A fate held in the hands of a man who detested me and a woman I barely knew.

I was not nearly as optimistic as Melody.

CHAPTER TWENTY SIX

Miller arrived early the next morning to review my testimony. He explained the hearing procedures and informed me he was unable to procure a defense, which did not surprise me. Luckily, I'd procured my own.

"What if the people I saved testify that I never alerted them to their impending deaths, and did nothing purposely to change the timeline to that end?"

He sat silently for several moments, pulling at his greying mustache.

"Sure, Charlie. It's worth a shot. But you're assuming they will both be available to testify."

"Victoria Weddington is on her way."

His eyes widened, obviously impressed by my ingenuity. "That still leaves your dad."

Heat rose to my face. "I didn't think *he* would be a problem, although to be honest, I haven't talked to him in days. I just assumed he'd attend his own son's hearing."

"He called my office yesterday to check in." He cleared his throat. "He's in New York today, doing the morning news circuit. He won't be here."

I pounded the table with my fists. "Call him. Tell him I need his testimony."

"He wouldn't make it in time. We have less than two hours until your appearance."

My mind raced. "Call him anyway. Have him send an email with his statement."

"It would need to be signed and notarized. An email won't be admissible."

I closed my eyes and felt the room begin to spin. The irony of my situation was not lost on me. My mother, who met me only twice, insisted on being present to defend me. My father, on the other hand, was off pursuing his own agenda to assure my 'criminal activity' would never reflect poorly on him.

I took a deep breath. "Fine. We don't need him. We'll just let my mother testify. Hopefully it will be enough to convince the board I didn't intend on breaking the law."

He slid his glasses down the bridge of his nose and rubbed his eyes. "If that's what you want, then that's what we'll do. Just know that I haven't had an opportunity to talk to her or review her testimony. I have no idea what type of witness she'll be. It's a crapshoot at best."

I couldn't believe his audacity. To arrive without a defense and then balk against the one I provided. It was no wonder my father hired him. My inclination was to fire him on the spot, but I knew it was not in my own best interest to defend myself.

"I'll take the crapshoot," I replied finally. "It's better than nothing, which is what you're providing."

He flinched at my disdain, but quickly regained his composure, repositioning himself in his chair while he tapped his papers curtly on the table.

"When they call us in, just let me present your case. They may or may not ask for you to speak on your own behalf. Is that something you feel comfortable doing?"

"Yes. Of course," I replied without hesitation.

"You may want to give it some serious thought," he said, massaging the back of his neck. "Look, Charlie, you're a nice enough kid. Clean cut. All-American. People love that stuff. They eat it up. But if you take the stand, you run the risk of saying something that will hurt your image. You don't want to sound like a pretentious know-it-all. Or a sarcastic brat. Or an entitled idiot. Not that you are any of those things, you just can't come off sounding that way."

"So how am I supposed to sound?"

"You have to be remorseful. Ignorant of your mistake. They have to truly believe that you intended on obeying the law."

"I *did* intend on obeying the law!"

He sighed. "Okay. I'll let you take the stand. And I'll let your mother take the stand as well. And I'll do my best to present you both in a way that conveys that you had no intention of saving anyone's life."

"Good."

"Yes. But remember, the board won't hesitate to ask tough questions. Are you prepared to answer them truthfully?"

"Yes!" I exclaimed, exasperated by his lack of understanding. "I have nothing to hide! I didn't intend on saving anyone's life!"

He didn't respond, and instead began shuffling through his files. He handed me a thick manila envelope containing an instruction manual.

"Here's a list of some of the questions they might ask, including appropriate responses." He checked his watch. "You don't have long before they'll call you to be sequestered prior to the hearing. Until that time, read through these. Try to memorize the answers. Knowing the proper way to respond will be the best chance you've got at earning a ticket out of here."

I took the file from his hands. "Why didn't you give this to me yesterday? Or the day before? How come I'm just getting it now?"

He rubbed his temples. I could tell he was counting to ten as he was clearly as frustrated with me as I was with him.

"You want the truth?"

"Yes. Of course."

"Your case is a long shot, kid. I haven't been here because I've been working with other clients who actually have a shot of winning."

His admission hit me like a punch to the gut, deflating my ego and defusing my anger in one fell swoop. My expression must have shown how deeply his words upset me as he quickly rescinded, patting me on the shoulder.

"But that doesn't mean you shouldn't try. Stranger things have happened, right? And you've got your mother's testimony I wasn't counting on, so who knows? You just might walk out of here after all." He attempted a smile, which may or may not have been genuine.

"Thanks," I replied. "I guess I'll get to work."

I spent the next hour reading over the manual. The answers felt robotic. Artificial and contrived. I quizzed myself, replying to each question truthfully and then comparing my answer to the suggested response. It was a disaster. The manual's answers were fact driven and concise. While the instructions suggested I explain the purpose of my trip using ten words or less, I droned on for three minutes, discussing my need for closure surrounding the death of my father and my biological mother. The more questions I attempted to answer, the more exasperated I became. Finally, I threw the book at the wall in frustration, and it hit the floor with a loud thud.

I was startled by an attractive brunette clearing her throat in the doorway. "Is everything okay, Mr. Johnson?" she asked.

I grabbed the manual from the floor and attempted to collect myself. "I'm fine."

There was a softness to her expression which led me to believe she was newly hired. Everyone else I encountered at the facility appeared weary. Almost cynical. She lacked that calloused exterior. "That's good," she said smiling, "because it's time for your hearing. Follow me, please."

I held tightly to the book as I fell in step beside her in the hallway. "Do you get to see a lot of these cases?" I asked.

"Not a lot. But some."

"Have you seen them let people off?"

"Only once or twice. But I haven't worked here that long."

We rounded a corner toward an unfamiliar section of the building. "How'd they do it?"

She slowed her pace to look up at me. "Do what? Get acquitted?" She shook her head. "I don't know. Sometimes there's not enough evidence. One time a guy was terminal. Had a couple weeks to live. That's not the case for you, is it?"

I smiled. "No. At least not that I'm aware of."

She stopped and turned to face me. Her voice was empathetic. "I don't think there's any magic bullet. No recipe for success. Just tell the truth. Your truth. At the end of the day, it's really all you have."

She was right. I tossed the manual in the trashcan as we reached the sequestration room. If I was going down, I was going down on my own terms, with my own truth.

She opened the door. "The bailiff will take you from here," she said. "Good luck."

I was sworn in by the officer in the small room adjacent to the main chamber. It was surreal, knowing that although my family waited just beyond the wall, the government prevented us from being together. Out of nowhere, desperation overpowered me, and my mind flooded with images of their lives continuing without me. I envisioned Melody accepting her diploma at her high school graduation, Brooke opening her own veterinary clinic, and my mother cradling grandchildren in her arms. Children who would not belong to me.

I couldn't lose them. I couldn't stand the thought of not being part of their lives. When he returned, the bailiff found me shaking in the metal folding chair in the corner of the room.

"Charles Johnson? Let's go," he announced, reading from his clipboard as he opened the door into the hearing chamber.

As I entered, my eyes had difficulty acclimating to the brightness of the room. Slowly, my vision adjusted, and I saw Miller look up to acknowledge me from behind a glass of water and a small stack of papers. His apathetic expression disquieted me. I knew the outcome of my case would have no bearing on his life, and therefore, he had no vested interest in seeing me released. Regardless of the ruling, he would return to his family at the end of the day. Anger raged within me as I took my seat beside him.

I turned around to scan the room until I found her, my beautiful Brooke, sitting bravely in front of her parents between my mom and

Melody, on one of the spectator benches in the back of the room. She appeared tired but her eyes were not bloodshot. It was obvious she hadn't been crying. I waved to her discreetly, and although she smiled, I knew it was only for my benefit. By maintaining her composure she was attempting to make me feel better about the possibility of a guilty verdict. Without consideration for herself, she was trying to be strong for me.

I did not deserve her.

With this admission, the truth of my situation shifted into focus with amazing clarity. I had no one to blame for my circumstances but myself. I couldn't be angry with Miller for his indifference, as he had absolutely nothing to do with the cause of my incarceration. The government officials I spent all week cursing for their lack of understanding were only trying to protect the public from ruining their lives. The very laws I chose to violate were the laws designed to guard us from ourselves. Even my father, whose self-serving decisions kept me from the truth and propelled me into action, could not be blamed for the end result.

Only my own selfishness was responsible for my current situation. Without Brooke's support, I coerced my mom into confessing the truth of my adoption. Then I convinced her to accompany me on the search for my mother, and was unyielding to her pleas regarding the use of my trip.

So now, as I sat before a delegation of men and women with the power to shape the direction of my future, I decided to take that power away from them. I promised myself I was done being selfish. I knew immediately that regardless of the board's ruling, I was going to let Brooke go.

She deserved her freedom. Freedom from a man who couldn't be trusted to put her needs before his own. Freedom from a man who was, at the end of the day, no better than his father. She, like my mothers, deserved better than I could give her.

As I allowed the peace of my decision to wash over me, the hearing got underway. The board read the charge against me and presented the evidence supporting the charge. Apparently the government keeps records of each person's individual timelines throughout the course of their lives. Evaluated only by computers, timeline monitoring modules detect glitches between various timelines and depending on certain criteria, alert officials. Unfortunately for me, the modules reported two glitches in my timeline, and based on the timing, officials easily identified my parents as the cause of the discrepancies. Miller spoke for several minutes in my defense, outlining the information we discussed, falling just short of begging outright for the board's leniency. And just when I thought I could no longer hold together the frayed edges of my composure, I was finally, mercifully, called to take the stand.

CHAPTER TWENTY SEVEN

The jury, consisting of seven board members of varying ages and ethnicities, sat at a semicircular table at the front of the chamber. I felt their scrutinizing gaze as I made my way to the chair opposite them in the center of the room. I scanned their faces, hoping some expression of empathy would pass between us. There was boredom, annoyance, and even contempt, but sadly, none of the men or women tasked with deciding my fate appeared to have been blessed with the gift of compassion.

I held my breath.

The chairman sat at the center of the table, staring at me disapprovingly.

"Tell us about your trip, Mr. Johnson."

My mind went blank. None of the questions in the manual were so vague.

I reminded myself to be truthful and concise. And to avoid sarcasm.

"What would you like to know?"

"Why don't you just start at the beginning," he replied. "Why did you decide to go back in time?"

Truthful. Concise.

"I recently found out I was adopted, and both my father and birth mother were deceased at that time. I went back to discover the truth about my adoption."

"Was there no one else who could have provided you with the

information you were seeking within the present timeline?"

Truthful. Concise.

"I attempted to discuss my adoption with my grandparents but they refused to speak with me."

"I see. How about during your trip? Did you discuss the matter of your adoption with your father in the past?"

"No."

"Did you discuss the matter of his death?"

"No."

"What did you discuss with your father?"

"Nothing. I avoided him, just as I did in the original timeline."

"So you are saying you changed nothing in the timeline that directly resulted in your father's life being saved?"

"Yes, that's what I'm saying."

He looked to his left and right at the other members of the board who were listening intently to his questioning. The woman beside him whispered in his ear. As they quietly conferred with one another, I heard the hinges of the rear chamber door creaking open. I turned to see Victoria crossing the threshold. She hesitated in the doorway.

"I'm sorry, Ma'am, but this is a closed hearing."

She held up a paper in her hand.

"The guard sent me here. Room 407, right? I'm supposed to be a witness for my son, Charlie Johnson."

"Ah, you must be Ms. Weddington. Take a seat. We'll be with you shortly."

Our eyes locked. Brooke understated the changes in her appearance since I last saw her. Her face was full, her eyes no longer sunken in their sockets. Her skin held a healthy glow, and as she smiled at me, I could feel her loving presence from across the room. She studied the handful of spectators, and was clearly relieved when she recognized Brooke and Melody. She hastily settled on the seat beside Brooke's father.

"Well, now that she's arrived, would you like to tell us about your birth mother?" the chairman asked.

"What about her would you like to know?"

"Did you discuss the matter of your adoption with her during your trip?"

"I did."

"But this was not something you discussed in the original timeline."

"No. It was not."

"So, for the record, you admit to making a change to the timeline with regard to discussion of your adoption with your birth mother?"

"Yes."

"Make a note, Ms. Winters," he said to the woman beside him. "Now, Mr. Johnson, what exactly did you discuss with your birth mother about your adoption that was different from the original timeline?"

Truthful. Concise.

"I wanted to find out what any person would want to know when they discover they're adopted. I needed to find out why I was given up for adoption. I wanted to know the circumstances." I felt my heart beating heavily in my chest as I finally acknowledged the one true motive for my search. "I needed to know if I'd been loved."

I heard the fluorescent lights humming above my head. Several board members shuffled uncomfortably in their chairs.

Out of nowhere, Miller chimed in. "I don't see how this line of questioning has any relevance to the case."

"Noted and overruled," the chairman responded without missing a beat. "Very well then, did you discuss the matter of your mother's death with her during your trip?"

"No."

"You gave no indication that her life was in peril?"

"No."

"You made no changes to her life to affect the outcome of the original timeline?"

"None that I'm aware of."

He thumbed through a stack of papers on the table in front of him. "Thank you very much, Mr. Johnson. That will be all. Please return to your seat. And Ms. Weddington, you can join us here in the front please."

As I stood up, I was reminded of getting lost in the woods on the far edge of town when I was eight. I ran for hours trying to find my way home and could barely lift my legs when I finally climbed the porch steps just before dark. My legs felt exactly the same way as I returned to my seat beside Miller.

As my mother passed beside me, she reached out and squeezed my arm. Her grip was strong. It was an act of solidarity, carrying with it the hopes and dreams of two decades lost in time.

The bailiff approached to swear her in and the questioning began.

"Ms. Weddington, I know you are unaware of what transpired in the original timeline that resulted in your death, so you will be unable to provide insight into the exact change that was made with regard to your life being saved. However, I would like to hear about the time you spent with your son on the dates in question. Were you aware that Mr. Johnson was using his trip during the time of your meeting?"

"No, I sure wasn't. He never said anything about that to me."

"Perfect. And what did he discuss with you when you met?"

She turned to look at me. Her hands were shaking. It was obvious she was nervous about getting me in trouble by saying the wrong thing. All I could do was smile in the hopes of conveying my faith and gratitude.

"He asked me about why I gave him up," she replied at last, "and I told him the truth."

"Which was?"

"Irrelevant to the case," Miller interrupted once again.

"Not so," the chairman snapped, glaring at my attorney. "We are looking to establish what the relationship was between Mr. Johnson and Ms. Weddington. Answer the question, Ms. Weddington."

"I gave him up because I was a junkie and Phil Johnson didn't want me to be the one to raise him," she said carefully, protecting the agreement she made with my father long ago.

"And how did Mr. Johnson react to hearing this information?"

"He was…" She wrung her hands in her lap, unable to continue.

"Ms. Weddington, answer the question."

She turned again to face me, tears in her eyes. "He was amazing. Kind and understanding. He forgave me for what I did."

The chairman slid forward in his seat. "And how did that make you *feel?*" he asked.

She hesitated. I felt the blood pulsing through the veins in my neck. I knew her response was about to shatter any hope I had of being released. Perhaps she knew it too.

"Better than any drug I ever took," she whispered.

"And what did you do after meeting with Mr. Johnson?"

"I went home."

"And after that?"

She sighed heavily. "I got clean."

"Well. Isn't that wonderful? Not only did you get clean, but you survived whatever tragedy was to befall you. That's a pretty lucky coincidence, don't you think?"

"Yes. Very lucky," she replied.

"Well then, I think those are all the questions I have for you today, Ms. Weddington."

She was on her feet, lunging toward the chairman before anyone in the room could react. Her carefully composed exterior gave way to the desperation she was holding inside. "You don't understand," she cried. "He never told me I was going to die! I didn't know there was anything I needed to avoid! Please, you have to understand, it was just a mistake!"

"Mistakes only happen when travelers make careless decisions. And Mr. Johnson made a careless decision by speaking to you. You are alive as a direct result of the actions he took during his trip. I'm sorry, Ms. Weddington. I know you were only trying to help." He turned to the bailiff. "Please see her out, Officer."

In what seemed like a foggy haze, I watched helplessly as the bailiff removed my grief-stricken mother from the room. The board members began whispering amongst themselves, and I felt Miller pat me on the back, a sign of consolation. As the minutes ticked by, I heard my family weeping quietly behind me, and yet I lacked the courage to turn and face them.

The chairman's voice pulled me from my daze. "Mr. Johnson, if you would please stand for our verdict."

I pulled myself up and braced myself against the table, unable to support my own weight.

"Charles Johnson, we find you guilty of saving two lives, a direct violation of the time travel code, section 17, article 2 during government sanctioned trip 396DIB92. As a result of this guilty verdict, we are sentencing you to fifteen years in a long term housing facility. You will be eligible for parole after ten years. Do you understand the sentence that is being handed down?"

"Yes," I replied.

"Good," he said, his callous demeanor unwavering. "Now I want to explain a few things to you, Mr. Johnson. You need to understand that men like you are the reason we specifically monitor travelers of your age and demographic. The federal government doesn't have the funding or manpower to follow the consequences of every trip, but you better believe we track young, rich men like yourself who have lived their entire lives thinking they are above the law. You and your highfalutin lawyer here could have dragged the Pope himself to testify on your behalf, and it wouldn't have made any difference. We need to make an example out of men like you to help save the lives of others. So to that end, thank you for your service. I'll allow you several minutes to speak with your attorney and family before the bailiff returns you to your cell."

Miller shook my hand and apologized for being unable to help me with the case. Before I could respond, he picked up his folio and was halfway to the door.

I remained standing, frozen as though my feet were cemented in the ground. I knew I had to face my loved ones, as well as my new reality, but I couldn't bring myself to acknowledge what had just transpired. I closed my eyes and counted to ten, hoping perhaps it was just a horrible nightmare.

Before I finished counting, I felt the presence of someone beside me. As I opened my eyes, my mom placed her arms around my waist and began to cry. She attempted to speak but her words became lost in the spasms which shook her body. I slipped my arms around her shoulders to console her as Melody approached me from the other side.

"It's all my fault," she sobbed. "I'm the one who had the idea about using your trip. I should go to jail, not you!"

"It's nobody's fault," I assured her. "It just happened. It's what was meant to be."

"You can't believe that," Brooke said, joining us in the center of the room with her puffy eyes and fists full of tissues.

I was numb. I didn't know what to believe anymore. I was certain I'd find fulfillment once I discovered where I came from, but sadly, in the quest to fill the void, I had inadvertently squandered every blessing in my life. I felt more empty and insecure than I ever had before. However, there was at least one thing I was sure of... I would not allow the people I loved to be destroyed along with me.

"Listen to me, all of you. You are my life. You've always been my life. I didn't know it before now, that you were all I ever needed, but now that I know, I can't stand the thought of destroying your lives along with mine. You must promise me you will go on. Promise me."

"But I need my brother!" Melody cried.

"I'll call when I can. You can visit when they allow. I can still be a part of your life," I told her. "You too, Mom."

"And what about me?"

I turned to face the woman I loved more than any other soul on the planet. "No, Brooke. Not you."

She lifted her chin and took a step closer, reaching out to touch me. But she resisted. "You told me once, the first time we met, when we were in high school, that you would wait for me. But I was cruel to you and you moved on. That's when you made me promise to never find you again, because you said it was too hard to say goodbye. And now, here we are. Another life. Another timeline. And you're asking me to walk away from you again? To go on with my life pretending I never met you? Pretending there was never *us*? Is that fair, Charlie?"

I reached down to brush a tear from her cheek with my thumb. "It's the only thing that's fair. In fifteen years, you'll be a vet with your own practice. You'll be married. You'll have children. You'll be living the life you were meant to live."

"I'll be miserable! I can't just 'unknow' you! I can't just pretend we never happened. I tried to do it before and it was excruciating. Don't ask me to do it again!"

"I'm not asking you, Brooke."

"Please, Charlie."

"I won't see you. I won't allow you in. I won't take your calls. This is the only gift I can give you that makes any sense. You deserve the chance at a normal life. You deserve to be with a man who will put your needs before his own. I'm not that man."

"You are!" she cried.

"I'm not." My throat felt thick from holding back tears as I struggled to maintain my composure.

Brooke's father came to her side and wrapped her in his arms. "I'm so sorry, Charlie," he said. "I'm sorry it had to end this way."

"I love you," she breathed.

"I love you, too," I replied.

Her mother and father led her out of the chamber through the back entrance. She didn't look back. It was better that way. She always said quick goodbyes were less painful.

CHAPTER TWENTY EIGHT

I looked for Victoria as the bailiff led me through the halls of the facility back to my basement cell. My heart ached for her, as our connection was now bound by gratitude as well as forged in blood. I needed her to know how much I appreciated her effort, and that I didn't blame her for the judgment. But sadly, she was nowhere to be found.

Less than an hour from the verdict, I was transported by van to the closest long term housing facility, otherwise known as prison. Everything happened so quickly, I was too stunned to appreciate the graveness of my situation, much less reflect upon the consequences I would soon face.

Upon arrival, I was processed and immediately indoctrinated into my new life in the facility. The building itself was divided into cell blocks, each with its own set of rules and brand of inmates. Due to the nonviolent nature of my crime, my cell was located in the least restrictive section. My ward consisted of 24 cells lining the perimeter of a large common area. During the day, we were allowed to pass unguarded between our cells and the shared space, which was comprised of several sofas, three televisions, a stack of well-worn board games, and a small library of books. There were also enough tables and chairs for each prisoner to have a seat during meals. Breakfast, lunch, and dinner were served off of compartmentalized trays, rolled in on large, metal carts by the staff. Each afternoon before dinner, we were taken to an outdoor recreation area complete with a weight bench, two treadmills, and a basketball net. At night, we were locked within our cells from 10 PM until 5:30 in the morning, when the day began, each one exactly like the last.

The first days of my incarceration were agonizing. I struggled to acclimate myself to prison life, with its mindless routine and unspoken codes of conduct. By keeping my head down and my ears open, I was able to navigate the complex hierarchy established by my fellow cell block inmates. There were seats that were off limits and television channels which were not to be changed. I learned who controlled the communication channels between the inmates and the wardens, and which prisoners were acceptable to approach with concerns. I stopped hoping to enjoy meals, realizing the tasteless food was meant only to supply empty calories, a means of keeping me alive and nothing more. I mastered the art of rolling my socks inside my ill-fitting shoes to alleviate the blisters which were already beginning to callous my feet.

By the end of the first month, I was fully assimilated into prison life. I successfully learned to navigate the murky waters of captivity. However, as I lay staring at the ceiling on the evening of my thirty-first day, I acknowledged the painful truth of my situation. Physically, I was enduring. Spiritually, I was dying swiftly every day.

Life inside the prison walls would have been horrendous enough if I'd been alone in the world, without memory of my family and friends. My heart ached to be with them, sharing activities that often went unappreciated in everyday life. I missed my classmates, teammates, and even my coworkers whose companionship I never fully appreciated. I dreamed about the simple act of grocery shopping with Mom, reaching the items on the top shelf and sneaking junk food into the cart while she wasn't looking. The thought of Victoria, alive and well in her newfound sobriety, left me longing for a relationship with her that would never come to pass. I thought of Melody, and all the milestones I would miss in her life. I wouldn't be there to interrogate the boys she dated. I wouldn't see her walk across the stage at her high school or college graduations. There was a good chance I'd never dance with her on her wedding day, and I might even miss getting to hold her firstborn child.

While it was difficult to speculate about how life continued on for most everyone outside the prison walls, I could not permit myself to dwell upon my greatest loss. Each time my mind would wander toward thoughts of Brooke, I would become physically and emotionally ill. My stomach churned. My heart raced. I dreamt about her almost every night. After several weeks of torment, I stopped allowing myself to think of her. I pretended she was dead to fool myself into believing her love was no longer a possibility.

Slowly, I began to numb.

In the darkest hours of the morning, I consoled myself with the hope they would each go on without me, finding their way in the world of which I was no longer a part. I knew in my heart they would survive, and perhaps even thrive, but it did little to dull the grief, the constant reminder of my poor decisions.

By the second month, I began reflecting upon the feelings of isolation which led me on the search for my mother initially. I recalled the first time I felt the hole in my life. When Melody was born, the change in our family dynamic was unmistakable to me. My mom looked at her in a way she never looked at me. It was subtle. Indistinguishable to everyone else. Perhaps it was merely a subconscious manifestation of the biological tie to Melody she did not share with me. Whatever the reason, I had felt from that moment that I didn't quite belong. Something was missing. I was smart enough to allow Melody, in her childhood naïveté, to help fill the empty space. But for every inch my sister filled, my father took back twice as much. I searched for love with the girls I dated in high school, but none could come close to approaching the depth of devotion my heart required.

Alone in my cell, with nothing but time to dwell upon my past, I realized the moment my mom confirmed my adoption was the moment I acknowledged the vastness of that void. I knew immediately that my parents' secrets were responsible for creating the hole inside me. When faced with the reality of no biological connections and more importantly, no knowledge of who my parents were or where I came from, it was no wonder I struggled to define my sense of self.

At the time, I thought I knew how emptiness felt.

As I considered my 15 year sentence, which destroyed life as I knew it, it seemed laughable that I had ever felt called to fill a void in my life. If I had realized how full of love it had actually been, I would have never considered risking it all by taking my trip. Feelings of self-loathing filled my days as I dwelled upon how the emptiness of the past paled in comparison to the depth of loss I now faced. In my effort to find myself, I shattered the hope of having normal relationships with everyone who helped shape my identity. Without them, I was irreparably damaged.

Lost beyond all hope.

The only joy in my life came in the form of Sunday visitation. Friends appeared initially to offer their support and understanding, but after several months passed, they stopped coming altogether. I didn't blame them. Regardless of their efforts, by the time I was released, I had no doubt we would be strangers. There was no sense in trying to pretend our friendships would sustain the hardship of prison. When the time came for me to reenter the world, I would begin again with a new set of friends.

My family, on the other hand, came to visit every Sunday. Mom and Melody arrived promptly at ten, the minute the doors opened, with news of the outside world and the occasional baked good. I never slept the night before, in anticipation of their arrival. My excitement was far too great. Unspoken rules were established early on regarding topics that were acceptable and those that were off limits. I loved hearing about the monotony of their daily lives; which new stores opened up in town, what books Mom was reading, how Melody was doing in algebra. There were only two topics they knew I never wanted to discuss: my father's campaign and Brooke.

Melody tried initially to work her into conversation, mentioning she saw her at the park or that Brooke took her to a movie. It broke my heart to know they were both still living the charade that their lives would remain entwined without me tying them together. I knew, however, Brooke would eventually move on, finding someone new to love. In time, she would spend her time with his family and in the end, Melody would be left behind. Another casualty caused by my string of poor decisions.

My father only came to see me four times. On each occasion, a film crew accompanied him to document our traumatic separation. During the final visit, when I refused to speak, he left without a word and did not return. It had been many weeks since I'd seen him. It was the only positive outcome of the new timeline.

Snow fell in the exercise courtyard on the date marking month four of my incarceration. The hollowness was now something which fully defined me. It was with me the moment I opened my eyes in the morning, and it stayed with me every second of the day. It was with me, gnawing at my insides as I sat looking into the sky, snowflakes sticking to my eyelashes and hair. Shivering in my threadbare coat, I conceded defeat to the destructive nature of the hunger for truth which destroyed me. And although that truth allowed me to briefly experience the love of the mother I never knew, its promise quickly faded to reveal what was ultimately most important in my life.

The people who loved me all along.

Mom. And Melody.

And Brooke.

I allowed myself to think of her for a moment. Her kindness. Her dedication. Her ability to magnify the beauty in the world by simply being alive. I prayed silently, that wherever she was, whatever she was doing, she was happy.

Then I folded my knees beneath my chin and covered my head with my arms.

And I cried.

PART FOUR

CHAPTER TWENTY NINE

The sun was shining through the window. It was unnaturally bright in the room. It snowed several inches the day before, and I attributed the brilliance of the day to the sun's reflection off the blanket of snow on the ground.

I switched off the television and perused the bookshelf for something new to read. I was between Patterson and Koontz when the doorbell rang.

"I got it," Melody yelled from the kitchen.

I listened as she skidded across the floor in the foyer. She was seeing Justin Taylor since before Thanksgiving, and I knew she was hoping he was stopping by to visit. It was amazing to see her transforming into such an incredible young woman, and I wasn't looking forward to leaving her behind when I returned to campus in less than a week to begin the second semester of my senior year.

"Charlie," she called, "it's someone for you!"

Brooke and I were meeting later in the day, and I knew winter break was already over for most of my other friends, so I couldn't imagine who was at the door. The book temporarily forgotten, I made my way into the foyer where I greeted an older gentleman wearing a weathered grey uniform.

"Can I help you?" I asked curiously.

"I'm looking for a Charlie Johnson. Is that you?"

"Yes. Can I ask what this is about?"

"Of course." He dug through his messenger bag and handed me a manila envelope. It was addressed to me but included no return address.

"I gotta tell you, this is the strangest delivery I've made in my life," he said as I began peeling back the adhesive on the flap. "I get a lot of requests for special deliveries... you know, anniversaries, birthdays, that kind of thing. But nothing quite like this. A woman showed up a few months ago with this envelope. She was just as nice as she could be. Pays the postage and then asks me not to deliver it. Says she wants me to wait until today. This date specifically. Then I was supposed to wait until noon for a phone call. If no one called me about it, then I was supposed to deliver the envelope this afternoon. Never got a phone call, so here I am. And there's your letter. Sure would like to know what all this is about. Guess it's none of my business though. I'm just the delivery guy."

I didn't know what to make of the envelope. Or the delivery man. I dug through my wallet for a tip, thanked him for his time, and closed the door.

"What do you think's inside?" Melody asked from around the corner where she'd been listening.

"I have no idea."

"Should I get Mom?"

"No. Come on," I said, leading her to the family room. "We can open it together."

Melody plopped beside me on the sectional, and I carefully slid out a piece of paper, torn from the pages of a spiral notebook.

It was a letter. Melody read with me over my shoulder.

Dearest Charlie,

After you came to find me, you changed my life. Knowing you forgave me for the decision I made, allowing your father and his wife to raise you was the most amazing gift you could have ever given me. In that moment, I knew I wanted to change my life so I could be something more for you. Something better. I got clean and sober. I started working. I moved into a halfway house and began attending NA and AA meetings every day. However, I was unaware that while I was cleaning up my life, I was changing the path of my timeline. A timeline I didn't realize you had already lived before.

I didn't die after you came to see me as you were expecting I would. Neither did your father. And because we didn't die as we had in the previous timeline, you were indicted, found guilty, and sentenced to 15 years in prison for saving my life during your trip. I was a witness at your trial but was unable to help keep you out of jail. I never got to say goodbye.

That's when I got the idea of using my trip.

I often thought about going back in time to make sure I never met your father. Without him around, I know my life would have taken a much different path. That path however, would not have included you. I could never bring myself to do it because I knew I would be taking you from the world. Then, while you were standing trial, you said that all you wanted during your trip was to discover if you were loved.

You saved my life, Charlie, but I couldn't let you ruin your life for me. After your trial, I enrolled in time travel classes. I passed the tests and went back in time to undo what you had done. I never stopped using drugs. I never attended meetings. If you're reading this letter it's because I've passed away, as I did the first time. I pray that what I've done will be enough to rewrite the future once again and keep you out of jail. I know your father may still be alive, but since there was no testimony against you related to him at your trial, I am hopeful they will let you off. I pray my death will come as it did before and that you will see at last that yes, you are loved. You always were. You always will be.

Love,
Mom

The letter trembled in my hands.

I read it a second time. And then a third.

"So after you used your trip, she didn't die. And dad didn't die either. And you were put in jail for saving them. Then she used her trip to try and put things back the way they were by dying again?"

My head was spinning. "Yeah."

"And since dad died again too that's why you never got in trouble?"

"I guess so."

She exhaled loudly through her teeth. "Jeez, Charlie."

I set the letter on the coffee table. "She died for me, Mel."

"She was supposed to die anyway."

"But then she didn't. She could have lived. And she purposely went back so that she would die and I would have a chance."

"She loved you."

"I barely knew her."

"It didn't matter. You were her kid."

I rubbed my eyes to keep from crying. Melody wrapped her arms around my neck.

"I should have spent more time with her. I should have tried to see her again."

"No, Charlie. You obviously did see her again. In the other timeline. And this is what she chose to do for you. This was her choice. Her decision. She did it because she loved you. And she knows you loved her back."

I stood up and began pacing the room. Melody was right. My mother was my savior.

"Fifteen years," I said.

"That's a long time."

"My life would have been over. I would have lost all of you."

"That's why she did what she did."

I couldn't believe how lucky I was to have been given a second chance. And then I remembered Brooke. With her I was given a third. I cringed at the thought of what she'd been through in the previous timeline. It had been over four months since I'd returned from my trip which meant we were separated for that amount of time in the augmented timeline. I was grateful neither of us had any memory of the pain we obviously suffered.

Suddenly, Melody spoke up. "So your mother kept doing drugs to ensure she would die. But that didn't have anything to do with Dad. Why didn't he survive?"

I stopped pacing, considering her observation.

"I have no idea. They both died in the original timeline. Then apparently, they both survived in the second. When she died again this third time, he died again too. That can't be a coincidence, can it?"

"It's weird for sure."

I checked my watch. Brooke and I were meeting later in the afternoon to volunteer at a cat adoption event at the pet store in town. I knew I couldn't wait that long to share the contents of the letter and its implications.

"I'm gonna head over to Brooke's. You wanna come?"

"Nah," she said. "I'm going to the ice rink with Justin and the others." She stood up to give me a hug. "I'm glad you're here, Charlie. I'm glad your mom saved you. Isn't it amazing when people surprise you with what they're capable of?"

I chuckled to myself. It certainly was amazing. Amazing didn't even begin to describe what it was. In my hour of need, she sacrificed everything for me. My heart swelled with equal amounts of joy and sorrow. It surprised me how closely tied the two emotions seemed to be.

I found Brooke making cookies with her mom. The unmistakable aroma of butter and sugar baking in the oven overpowered me as I let myself through the back door.

"You're here early!" Brooke exclaimed as I took off my coat and scarf, throwing them across the back of a kitchen chair.

"My cookie sensors went off, alerting me to nonnutritive homemade deliciousness. I'm kind of like Spiderman mixed with Betty Crocker," I replied, popping one of the snickerdoodles off the cooling rack into my mouth.

"You know where the milk is," her mom said, motioning toward the refrigerator. "Help yourself."

After pouring myself a glass of milk, I polished off half-a-dozen cookies while listening to Brooke and her mom arguing over which contestant would be kicked off their favorite reality TV show that night. When the last of the cookies came out of the oven, I helped her wash the bowls, spoons and measuring cups, and her mom headed to the grocery store. As soon as we were alone, I wasted no time telling her about the letter from my mother.

"Did you bring it with you?" she asked.

"Of course. It's in my coat pocket," I replied, returning the clean cookie sheet to the cabinet above the refrigerator. "You can read it."

She laid her dish towel on the table and fished through my jacket until she found the letter. I watched her face as she read its contents. I was unsure about how she would react to its many repercussions.

"Oh, Charlie," she said at last, looking at me with an expression of utter disbelief.

I sat down at the table beside her. I didn't say anything. I knew it would be better if I just let her think it through. She reread the letter a second time and didn't speak for several minutes.

"So I guess things didn't go as well as we thought they did."

"No," I replied. "I must have screwed something up with Victoria. I guess I gave her hope. Something to live for. I can't say I'm entirely sorry for that. At least if she died, she died knowing she was loved. That's better than the first time, right?"

"That's one way of looking at it." She began reading a section of the letter for a third time. "You were imprisoned, Charlie. Sentenced to fifteen years. That's crazy."

"Yeah. Really crazy. I figure, based on the timing, I probably spent about four months locked up."

She rested her head in her arms on the table and I could tell she was reflecting on the implications of the letter. "I wonder what I did?" she mused.

"I don't know. I'd like to think I would have let you go." I slid her off her chair and onto my lap.

"What makes you think I would have let you?" she said, resting her head in the crook of my neck.

"I would have made you. Fifteen years is a long time." I held her tightly. "We don't have to worry about it now though. Everything is as it should be."

As we sat together, I became aware that my breathing slowed to match the steady rise and fall of her chest. In that moment, the magnitude of Victoria's gift revealed itself to me in the simple joy of being able to wrap my arms around the woman I loved. Although I had no memory of losing her, it struck me as poignantly beautiful that she was still fully present in my life.

I didn't move or speak, relishing the moment. I knew she was digesting the news of my mother's sacrifice, and waited patiently to see if she would pick up on the strange coincidence of my parents' deaths. I knew she would eventually, and after several minutes of silent contemplation, she turned to face me.

"Victoria died and your dad died. Victoria didn't die and your dad didn't die. Victoria died and your dad died."

I grinned at her.

"That's not something to smile about," she said.

"I'm not smiling about that. I'm just smiling about how well I know you."

"How well do you know me?"

"Well enough that I was just wondering how long it was going to take for you to put the pieces together."

She cocked her head to the side and narrowed her eyes. "You may think you know me, but I am full of mystery and intrigue."

"You're like an open book," I replied, poking her in the ribs.

She squealed and jumped off my lap. "Stop, Charlie! Just be serious for two seconds! This is a big deal! Why would their deaths be connected?"

"I have no idea," I said, standing up to grab another cookie off the counter. "But the letter said there was no specific evidence linking me to my father's life in the second timeline. Only that they were able to directly trace my mother's life to changes I made."

"But come on… there has to be a connection."

"I think so too."

"Because the only change in the third timeline was caused by Victoria. You didn't know what was going on so you couldn't have changed anything that would have resulted in your father's death.

"Exactly. But he's dead, just the same."

"So when she dies, he dies?"

"But he died in a freak climbing accident, the same as he did the first time. How does that have anything to do with my mother?"

"I don't know. Maybe we need to find out."

CHAPTER THIRTY

I bolted upright in bed. Moments before, I'd been having a vivid nightmare about climbing a mountain with friends. I caught my foot in a crevice and was dangling off the side of a cliff, struggling desperately to free myself before finally waking up. Amazingly, within the context of the dream, my subconscious pieced together the connection between my parent's deaths.

Without stopping to put on a robe, I slipped quietly out of my bedroom and crept downstairs to my father's office. The door was unlocked, just as it had been the only other time I ventured inside on the afternoon of his funeral in the original timeline. The door groaned on its hinges.

I switched on the lights.

The box was still there, but it was no longer in the corner where I left it in the original timeline. At first I thought someone had moved it, but then I realized I never explored the room the second time, and it was still sitting beside the door where the police dropped it off. Of course, there was no need for snooping, because I already knew the secrets the office contained.

I emptied the contents of the box onto the floor and dug through the ropes. The fittings were the same. The anchors were tied in the same dangerous fashion. It dawned on me that if I'd wanted to, I could have easily prevented my father's death by alerting him to the faulty anchors. But if I had told him and he'd survived, I would have ended up incarcerated for my actions. I felt the tiniest pang of sadness as I considered his death. And then I remembered the reason why I ventured into the office in the first place.

My father's anchor was tied incorrectly. When it failed, he plummeted to the bottom of the ravine and died. Someone must have tampered with his equipment.

That person, whoever it was, killed my father. And I didn't believe it was a mistake, given that my father's death appeared to be directly connected to my mother's. With that information, there could only be one person responsible.

I sat on the floor of the office and worked through scenarios in my mind. I was certain Victoria's parents had something to do with my father's death. However, there were several things that just didn't add up. Victoria admitted lying to her father about Phil Johnson being responsible for her pregnancy, but somewhere along the line, he must have come to know the truth. I had no idea what catalyst caused Weddington to suspect my father after so many years, but Victoria's death must have been part of it.

After hours of obsessive contemplation, I finally accepted there were gaps in my theory which could only be filled by Weddington himself. I knew because of his age, he could not have been the one to tamper with the rigging, so he must have hired someone to go along on the trip with my father. The list of witnesses to his death was my one and only lead.

After repacking the equipment and retrieving the picture of my mother from my father's desk drawer, I returned to my room and began digging through my closet for the suit I wore to his funeral. In the pocket, right where I left it, was the business card given to me by the officer who'd been assigned to investigate my father's death. I hoped he would be able to provide me with the names of the people who accompanied my father on the trip.

As soon as I thought she was awake, I called Brooke. Like every Sunday morning, she was preparing for church with her parents, but she happily invited me over for our traditional Sunday dinner. Although I was bursting at the seams to tell her about my suspicions, I knew it was something we needed to discuss face to face.

My next phone call was to Detective Roger Sloot of the local sheriff's department. I explained my interest in speaking to the other members of my father's expedition to gain closure regarding his death. Within fifteen minutes, he emailed me the list consisting of eleven men. I recognized several of the names, but a few were unfamiliar. Of course, I didn't plan on speaking with any of them. Instead, after breakfast with Mom and Melody, I sat with my tablet at the kitchen table cross-referencing the names of the men on the list with members of Weddington's inner circle. I searched employee files, campaign photos, press releases, and public records. I was about to give up and head to Brooke's, when I clicked on a photo of a press junket and noticed everyone in the photo happened to be tagged.

Buddy O'Leary stood behind him, partially obscured by the podium. In addition to being with him in the photograph, he was also on the list of people who accompanied my father on the climb. The confirmation that someone close to Weddington witnessed my father's death fueled my investigation into overdrive.

I did a quick search for Buddy O'Leary, and found that he was employed as part of Weddington's security detail for many years. Additionally, he was an active member of the Vertical Rock Climbing Club of central Virginia. It was widely known that my father was an avid climber who hosted many mountaineering events over the years. With Weddington's political connections, it would have been relatively easy for him to have gotten O'Leary an invitation for the trip.

I printed out what I discovered and took it with me to Brooke's, hoping that together we could figure out what to do with the new information. Although I usually spent Sunday afternoons watching football with her father, as soon as we were finished eating, I escaped with Brooke to the kitchen where we washed dishes together instead.

"I think I know what happened to my father," I began.

She sighed. "You've said that three times already this week. Do you have an actual lead or just another hunch?"

Although she was right, I rolled my eyes anyway. "I got to thinking that the only people I know of tied to both my mother and father are her parents."

"Why would they kill your dad? That's crazy."

"I don't have that piece figured out yet, but I have a possible connection."

"What sort of connection?" she asked, scrubbing out the casserole pan.

"I found out this guy who is one of Weddington's henchmen was with my dad on the climbing trip when he died."

She set the pan in the sink and turned to face me. "You're kidding."

"No. I think he had this guy Buddy O'Leary tie my father's anchors to make the fall look like an accident. He's a member of a mountaineering club. He would have known how to redo them so they'd fail."

She abandoned her dishes and sat at the table, scrunching her face at me. "But why? Why kill your dad after all these years?"

"I don't know, but it has to be related to her death. You said yourself, 'when she dies, he dies.' That's all I've got to go on."

She grinned at me. "You figured all this out on your own. I'm impressed. Are you trying to steal my position?"

"What position?"

"As Sherlock, of course. Am I being relegated to Watson?"

"Never! That's why I'm here! I'm stuck. I need your help."

"Really?" she said, standing up to join me with the drying. "Well, first, you should know it's gonna cost you."

"Naturally," I grinned at her.

"But more importantly," she continued, "I need to know why I should help you on another one of your adventures. Truly, Charlie, we just discovered what a fiasco you made of the last one. Why bother with any of this? Maybe you should just let it go."

She was right, of course, and yet I needed for her to understand how I felt.

"I know there's no reason to investigate further. I get that. The police closed his case months ago, and nothing I might discover will bring him or my mother back. But I don't know if I can live with myself knowing my biological grandfather abandoned my mother, murdered my father, and never answered for any of it. I never stood up to my father for the way he treated me, just as my mother never stood up to her father. I think it's time to end the vicious cycle."

I tossed my towel on the counter and gathered Brooke into my arms. She felt solid. Grounded.

"This whole thing started because I was lost. I've always been lost. I've always felt like everyone else was in on this big secret I was never a part of. And it wasn't because I wasn't loved, because I was. But from early on, I realized something wasn't right." I swallowed hard, remembering the emptiness. "When I met you, for the first time in my life, all that stuff didn't matter as much. You knew what it was to feel lost, and you continued to thrive. You gave me hope that I could feel that way too. But then the possibility of finding my mother came along, and it was like a drug I couldn't pass up. When I found her and she told me my story, all the jumbled up pieces of my life fell into place. I can't explain why it was so important for me to do what I've done, but now that I have, I owe it to my mother to see this through to the end. Her father treated her worse than my father treated me. I can never forgive him for that. And now I think he may have had my father killed. He's a bad man, Brooke. He's cruel. Heartless."

"Like a tin man," she interrupted.

"Exactly. Like a tin man," I agreed. "And now I have the opportunity to see justice served. To make him understand he can't do whatever he wants and get away with it." I paused, resting my chin on the top of her head. "My mother died to save me, Brooke. I keep thinking that there's a reason why I'm here and she isn't. Maybe this is the reason why. Maybe this is what I'm supposed to do."

She pulled away, peering up at me with an expression of genuine love and understanding. "You need to confront him."

"He won't even see me. Remember, I tried before."

"It might be time for an ambush," she grinned.

Her smile was infectious. "I like the way you think, woman. What do you have in mind?"

"You want to get him to admit what he did, right?"

I shook my head. "Yeah. Good luck with that."

"It might not be as hard as you think, Charlie. We're dealing with a man who has the same personality type as your father. How would you have gotten him to admit something?"

I learned as a child how easy it was to manipulate him. When I was seven, I outgrew my training wheels and fell in love with an amazing BMX in the bike shop window across from school. When I initially mentioned it to my father, he told me it was a waste of money. Dejected, I returned to the store where I noticed a flyer advertising a father/son bike race. I took one of the race pamphlets home and left it on the kitchen counter for him to find. The next morning, when I noticed him looking at the paper, I commented that I thought there would be lots of people and maybe even camera crews at the event, and since he was such a great biker, he would probably win. Then I hung my head, bemoaning the fact that it would be fun for us to do together, but since my bike was too small, I wouldn't be able participate. The following day, he took me to the bike store, bought the BMX, and signed us up for the race.

"If it was my father, I'd stroke his ego, make him think whatever I wanted was his idea, and convince him he knew more than I did. He used to hate feeling like he wasn't in control."

"Do you think the same thing would work on Weddington?"

"Probably." I raised my eyebrows at her, giving her a look of uncertainty. "So what you want to do is show up and sweet-talk him into admitting he had my father killed?"

"Yes. And record it for evidence."

I shook my head. "I thought for sure you would tell me to go to the police."

"They'd never believe you."

"I know." I paused. "So are you gonna help me or not?"

She took my face in her hands, pulling me close to press her lips against mine. "Let's do this," she said.

CHAPTER THIRTY ONE

Three days later, my hidden recording device disguised as a flash drive arrived in the mail. Brooke secured a fifteen minute appointment with Weddington at his DC office for later in the week. Under the guise of a campaign manager intern, she charmed her way into an interview with the grace of an Academy Award winning actress. I had never been so proud.

We spent our final days of winter break holed up together planning the course we hoped her conversation with Weddington would take. I did a bit more research on O'Leary, confirming my suspicions he was capable of murdering my father. Although never found guilty, he'd been arrested several times for assault and weapons violations over the course of many years. He was a member of Weddington's staff for just over nine years, demonstrating a mutual respect and trust between the two men.

As Brooke and I drove together along route 211 toward DC, I struggled to discern why Weddington had my father killed. I knew how, by whom, when, and where; I just couldn't figure out why Victoria's death triggered him to have my father murdered. Especially given his estrangement from her. Something must have happened.

To avoid parking downtown, we stopped in Fairfax County and took the orange metro line into the Federal Center station. From there, it was only a short walk to Weddington's office. Along the way, we discussed everything but what we were about to do. We were as prepared as we were going to be, having been over the different scenarios dozens of times. All that was left to do was confront him.

At quarter of two, we stood on the front steps of the Rayburn House Office Building where Weddington and his staff were housed while Congress was in session. The wind cut at our cheeks, and Brooke blew into her hands to warm them.

"Are you nervous?" I asked, grabbing her hands and rubbing them between my own.

"Yes!" she responded. "I don't want to screw this up for you. It's a lot of pressure, Charlie."

I tucked a loose lock of hair under her knitted snow cap. "There's no pressure at all. Just do the best you can. If you can't break him, you can't break him. At least we tried. Worst case scenario, we turn over what we have to the police and let them try to figure it out."

She sighed. "You have my notes?"

"For the hundredth time, they're right here in the back pack. You have the recorder?"

"Here in my pocket. You have the earpiece?"

"Front pocket, with the car keys."

She shifted from side to side, out of nervousness or in an attempt to keep warm, I couldn't tell which. I checked my phone. It was almost 2 o'clock.

"Let's go inside and find his office. We don't want you to be late."

Inside the lobby, we inquired about a restroom, where Brooke fixed her hair and touched up her lipstick, and I secured the earpiece which would allow me to listen in on her conversation with Weddington as it was being recorded. When she emerged, looking particularly beautiful, her cheeks still rosy from the cold air, I handed her the notebook from the backpack.

"You ready?" I asked, gently brushing her face with my fingertips.

"Yes," she replied resolutely. "Now let's get up there before I lose my nerve."

We found the elevators and headed to the fourth floor. In the relative privacy of the elevator, I bent down to kiss her, hoping to convey my appreciation for what she was about to do.

"For luck," I said.

She repaid me with the warmth of her smile. "I may need more than luck," she replied as the doors slid open. "I feel like I could throw up."

"You're not gonna throw up. You'll be amazing." I scanned the length of the hallway. There were benches lining either side. "If I sit out here I should be able to hear what's going on." I pulled her into my chest and held her tightly. "You're one special girl, Brooke Wallace."

"I never get tired of hearing that, so just keep telling me, okay?" she replied, as she backed away toward the office with Weddington's nameplate on the door. From my earpiece, I heard the click of the recording device being turned on from within her pocket as she stepped inside. For better or worse, there was no turning back.

Weddington greeted her several minutes later. "How do you do, Miss Wallace?"

"I'm fine," she replied. "Thank you for allowing me the opportunity to speak with you today."

"It's my pleasure. Always happy to help a young woman on the track to a career in politics. Please, have a seat."

The audio muffled as the recorder shifted in her pocket. I heard papers shuffling and knew she was bringing out her notes. Out of habit, I crossed my fingers, smiling to myself at how ridiculous I must have looked.

"Where would you like to begin?" he asked.

She coughed nervously. "Representative, you are one of the preeminent politicians of our time. You've initiated and passed legislation on everything from social security reform to raising minimum wage to clean air initiatives. It seems that everything you do has such a positive effect on our society. What do you think your greatest accomplishment as a congressman has been?"

She delivered her lines flawlessly, with just the right inflection of reverence to boost his ego. He droned on for several minutes about how wonderful he was. I imagined the look on his face, resembling my father at the podium, speaking to his adoring constituents. Now I was the one who felt ill.

As we rehearsed together, Brooke asked him several more questions regarding effective campaign strategies and marketing.

"You certainly have worked your way into the public's hearts," she gushed.

"Well, that's mighty kind of you to say, Miss Wallace."

"I have a few more questions, if you don't mind. I know we're running short on time."

"I've certainly got a few more minutes for a pretty girl like you."

Neither spoke for several seconds. I could feel Brooke gathering her courage.

"I'm sure your daughter enjoyed hearing that when she was a child."

More silence. I held my breath. This was it.

"I'm sure she did," he replied at last.

Brooke continued. "There's very little in the media about your family, Congressman. Certainly they helped shape the vision of your platform and have supported your campaigns throughout the years. Can you tell me a little about how your personal life is affected by your position?"

"I would prefer not to discuss my family."

"Oh. I understand." Her voice wavered slightly.

I couldn't sit any longer and began pacing the hall.

"It's just that I read somewhere that your daughter passed away not too long ago, and I was so intrigued by your strength. It was as if you were unaffected, even though I'm certain losing her was devastating. Is there a secret to how you are able to compartmentalize your life so that personal matters don't interfere with the work you do for the good of this country every day?"

I could feel the tension in the room.

"What exactly did you read about my daughter?"

"Just that she died of a drug overdose." She paused. "Clearly, the drug epidemic in this country knows no boundaries. If someone with a father as astute and dedicated as you becomes an addict, it seems to me there's an obvious breakdown in drug enforcement. I assume it will be a concern you'll be addressing in your next term."

"Yes. Of course," he stammered.

"It must have been awful for you, knowing what she was going through. I'm sure you tried to help the best you could, but I know how it is. I watch those television shows about addiction. You can only help someone who wants to be helped, right?"

"Yes. Precisely."

I could hear Brooke's confidence building. "Usually on those shows, something bad happens that sends the person down the path of addiction. There's always a death or a divorce or some sort of abuse. A catalyst, you know? I can't imagine it was anything you would have known about. That must have been difficult."

"It was very hard. Nothing my wife or I were involved in, naturally. There happened to be one particular man who ruined her life, just like you said. After he led her astray, we were unsuccessful in bringing her back to us. A tragedy, truly. We tried to keep the matter private. I'm surprised you came across anything about her."

"Well, like I said, there's very little information out there. Anyway, I'm so sorry for your loss, Mr. Weddington. I hope the man was eventually brought to justice for what he did to your daughter."

"He was. He certainly was. Thank you for your concern."

I heard Brooke chuckle thinly. "I like to think if it was my dad, he would have killed the guy. I hope you don't mind me saying that, but my dad would do anything for me. Still calls me 'pumpkin' to this day. I'm sure it was the same with you and your daughter, but you know, since you're in the public eye, it's not like you can just go around taking care of things for yourself."

"You'd be surprised what I can do."

"Really?" She giggled. "Oh, I believe you. You have so much power and influence. I bet if you wanted to take care of that guy, he'd be taken care of for sure."

I heard the feet of a chair scraping across the floor. "Let's just say the man who hurt my daughter is no longer with us."

"My goodness, you are a courageous father. I guess it wouldn't be too hard for someone like you to get rid of some common thug though."

"This guy was no thug."

Brooke gasped. "Really?"

"No. He was a pretty big deal. But of course, I wasn't directly involved in his... retribution. I have people to take care of that sort of thing."

"Of course you do." I could hear her shuffling papers once again. "You needed someone with better climbing skills than you possess."

I feared my heart would explode from my chest.

"I beg your pardon."

"Climbing skills. You don't know the first thing about mountaineering with all the ropes and carabiners... and anchors."

"I'm not quite sure to what you're referring," he said matter-of-factly.

"Sure you do. It's pretty convenient that your bodyguard, Buddy O'Leary, is a member of the Vertical Rock Climbing Club. He knew exactly how to rig Johnson's anchors so they'd fail. That was pure genius. The only thing I still don't understand is why you blamed him for Victoria's death? What do you think he did to her?"

The microphone recorded dead silence. Not even the sound of breathing. I stopped pacing and pressed the earpiece further into my ear, listening for something, anything, to come out of the room. Just as I was about to burst into his office, I heard a loud thud, like the sound of fists being pounded onto a table.

"Who sent you here?" Weddington spat, his voice laced with fear and condemnation.

"No one sent me."

"You're a liar!" he yelled. The waver in his voice suggested he was coming unhinged. I only hoped she stroked his ego firmly enough that he felt safe exposing her to the truth.

"I'm not going to say anything to anyone," Brooke replied timidly. "I just wanted to know why. Your story fascinates me."

I heard a crash, like something had fallen. Or been thrown. I was suddenly worried for Brooke's safety and began moving toward the door.

"You want to know why?" he growled. "I'll tell you why. That bastard, Phil Johnson, got my girl pregnant and then ran off, that's why!"

"That was 20 years ago," she replied. "Why kill him off now?"

"I didn't know it was him back then! After having the baby, she turned to drugs. Never came back home. When she overdosed, the guilt almost destroyed me, knowing I wasn't there for her all those years. And then I saw the kid."

"Charlie?"

"Yeah. Charlie. Noticed him with his father at some charity event. I try not to pay much attention to other people's families, but something about him gave me pause. Maybe it was his eyes or his hair color. Who knows?" He hesitated and I held my breath, waiting for him to continue. "I spent the entire night trying to figure out what was so familiar about him. I don't know why I didn't see it right away. Maybe I didn't want to see it, but when I finally allowed myself to acknowledge his resemblance to my daughter, I confronted the piece of garbage about it. Johnson admitted everything. Then he talked about what a whore my daughter was." He was silent for a moment. "He didn't deserve to live," he concluded.

I heard Brooke breathing heavily. She had done amazingly well under pressure, getting all the information we needed to convince the police to reopen the investigation of my father's death. Now it was time for her to get out of there.

"I'm so very sorry to have upset you, Mr. Weddington. I appreciate your time. I'm happy to see myself out." There was static as the recording device in her pocket jostled about.

"Oh, no. Not quite yet, Miss Wallace. You need to understand something before you leave here this afternoon."

"Oh?"

"You need to remember who you are dealing with. I am a very powerful United States Congressman. My pockets are deep, as are my connections. No one in Washington will believe anything I've told you and neither will anyone else. You are in way over your head with your little investigative reporting stint. So I would suggest you move on and pretend this meeting never happened."

"Of course. I understand. I have no intention of speaking to anyone."

"I'll deny anything you say. And who do you think people will believe? A beloved civil servant or a nosy teenager?"

"You have my word. I'll never speak of this to anyone. Again, I apologize for interfering and I thank you for your time. I'll see myself out."

I began walking toward the elevator, distancing myself from Brooke in the event Weddington should follow her out the door. I turned the corner and sent her a quick text, letting her know I would meet her outside at the corner of the building.

She hadn't turned off the microphone, and I could hear her panting as she took off down the hallway. I was already in the lobby when she texted her reply, *C U there*. By then, we were too far apart for the recording device to adequately transmit the sounds of her departure. I watched discreetly from the street corner, my hood pulled over my head, for her to arrive. The seconds ticked by, each one seemingly longer than the one before.

At long last, I saw her scurry down the front steps and turn in my direction. Our eyes connected. She was scared. I slowed my pace, crossing the street in the direction of the Metro station. In less than a block, I felt her beside me.

"Keep walking," she said. "He might be following me."

"I gathered. That's why I got out of there."

As we reached the next corner, she headed north on 3rd Street towards the Capitol building.

"The Metro station is the other way," I told her.

"I'm not headed to the Metro," she said. "We're going to the police, and we're going there now."

CHAPTER THIRTY TWO

An hour later, we were seated in Lieutenant Paul Grimes' office, whose desk was littered with stacks of files and empty soda cans. Officer Grimes remained silent as he took our statements but seemed very interested in listening to the recording of Weddington and Brooke's conversation.

"I just pulled your father's report from the local sheriff's department where the accident occurred. It looked like a pretty open and shut case. What made you think to go after Weddington for this?"

I quickly decided to leave out any mention of time travel or my mother. "The police returned all my father's gear, and I noticed all the anchors were tied in a way that could cause this sort of tragedy. I knew he wouldn't have made those mistakes. I began to suspect someone else had tampered with his equipment. It took me a while to figure out who it was. After I was told about my adoption and learned Weddington and I were related, the pieces started falling into place. In the end, he was the only one who made sense."

"Well," said Grimes, "you've done some good investigating. Let's hear what you've got."

He clicked the thumb drive into his tablet and pressed play on the audio file. We relived the recent conversation, and I watched Brooke's face as their exchange grew more heated. She cringed as we listened to their confrontation, and I touched her tentatively on the knee. She took my hand, holding it tightly as though she feared Weddington was about walk through the door. When the recording ended, the officer shook his head while massaging the back of his neck.

"I suppose you two know what you've got here?"

I exchanged a sideways glance with Brooke and shrugged my shoulders.

"No, sir," I replied. "What do we have?"

"You've got yourself a one-way ticket to an all-out media circus, that's what you've got. It always amazes me how arrogant some of these politicians are, thinking they're above the law, and that no one will have the guts to stand up to them. Nobody in this town probably would have, to be honest. Sometimes all it takes is somebody with nothing to lose to discover the truth."

His words reverberated in my mind. It seemed ironic he thought I was someone with the freedom to do whatever I wanted, immune to the consequences. Nothing could have been further from the truth. Since the moment my father died, I was constantly reminded of just how much I had to lose. I knew, as far as Brooke and I were concerned, we'd avoid being a part of any further investigation. I wouldn't allow either of us to risk the third chance we were given. I squeezed her hand tightly and gave her a wink.

"I think we'd both like to sidestep the media circus, if you think that's possible."

He thought for a moment, filing our statements in an envelope. "I think if this goes to trial, it will be hard to avoid. But with evidence like this," he said, holding up the thumb drive, "I think our illustrious congressman might just settle out of court and quietly accept a plea bargain. We have a 'one-party consent' statute here in DC, so this should be admissible as evidence. We'll have to see how it all plays out."

Brooke fidgeted in her seat. "Should we be concerned for our safety?" she asked.

"I'll be sending officers to arrest him immediately so I don't think you'll have anything to worry about. He'd be a fool to send someone after you. You're certainly free to go, and I'll contact you if I need something more. And don't hesitate to call if there's ever anything you should need from me."

Without another word, she was on her feet. "Thank you very much for your time today, Officer," she said, shaking his hand.

We said our goodbyes, and after a quiet ride on the metro, we were back in my car on our way home.

It was difficult to concentrate on the traffic bottlenecking around us as we left the city. Brooke hadn't spoken a word since leaving the police station, and as she rested her head against the window, I was beginning to think the intensity of the day had been too much for her.

"You were amazing this afternoon," I said.

"I'm glad I could help."

"I never could've done what you did today. Without you, Weddington would have gotten away with murder."

"He still might."

"He won't."

She fell silent once again.

"You know what else? Without you, I never would have met my mother."

"I'm glad I could help," she responded again, somberly.

I reached across to poke her on the shoulder. "Heck, without you, I don't know that I would have ever found the courage to ask about the adoption. You found the picture, found my mother, took me to find her in the past..."

"I'm no saint, Charlie," she interrupted. "I only did it all because I love you. You'd do the same for me."

I brushed her hair from in front of her eyes. "I probably would. The difference is that you've never asked me to because you're so much more cautious than I am. But that's about to change. No more trips. No more adventures. No more Sherlock and Watson. Just plain, ordinary life. How does that sound?"

"Honestly?" She grinned at me. "It sounds horrid."

"What?"

"I'm serious. That's not who you are. That's not who *we* are. It may not always work out the way we want it to, but life's not about sitting on the sidelines. It's about doing what you were meant to do and being who you were meant to be. Now that you know who you are, Charles William Johnson, illegitimate son of the deceased Victoria Weddington and Phillip Johnson, adopted son of Karen, amazing half-brother to Melody, and grandson to a crazy assassin congressman, you can go about the business of being exactly who you're supposed to be."

"Grandson of a crazy assassin, huh?"

"Yup." Her eyes sparkled mischievously.

"I sound amazing. But you forgot the most important thing about me."

"What's that?"

I reached for her hand and interwove her fingers between mine, knowing I was exactly where I was supposed to be. "I'm the lucky guy who gets to love the amazing Brooke Wallace."

EPILOGUE

There were bugs everywhere and I was beginning to question my sanity. I smacked another mosquito biting my calf as we crossed the creek.

Brooke swatted the air, walking through a swarm of gnats. "Ugh, Charlie! What would possess you to make a three-hour drive back here for a hike the day before your graduation? I can't believe I haven't learned my lesson with you."

"You love this place."

"I love it in October. In January. In March. But May? Between the bugs and the poison ivy, I can honestly say this is definitely your dumbest idea to date."

"Dumber than the time I tried to go ice fishing and fell in?"

"No. That was pretty stupid," she said, as she attempted to free her t-shirt from a thorny shrub.

I slapped a mosquito off the back of her arm.

"What about when I took you to that secluded beach with the great swimming?"

She rolled her eyes. "The one with all the jellyfish? Yeah, that was a good time."

I laughed at her sarcastic tone. "So, see, by comparison, what are a few bugs?"

She sighed heavily. "It's not just the bugs, Charlie. It was three hours here, and we'll have another three hours back... I don't know why we couldn't have just done this next week, after we're home for summer vacation?" She paused. "Or at least I am."

We reached the falls and our picnic spot in record time. I brought along a blanket, which I laid along the riverbank, just close enough for us to take off our shoes and put our feet in. As I sat down, she plopped down heavily beside me and rested her head on my shoulder.

"It is nice here," she relented, stomping an ant with her shoe.

"It is."

She sat motionless, staring at the falls. "I can't believe you're graduating already."

"It was a crazy year. It went by fast."

"And now everything is about to change."

"For the hundredth time, I'm not leaving you."

"The Global Freedom Center is in Arlington. That's a long way from home. It's a long way from school."

"It's an amazing fellowship though. And it's just for a year. Think of all the people I'm going to be able to help."

"But vet school's in Blacksburg."

"So maybe I'll join you there when you start. Get my graduate degree in social work or criminal justice. Who knows what's going to happen over a year from now?" I turned her face from the falls to look at her properly. There were tears in her eyes. "It's all going to work out."

"How can you be so sure? Life is so... complicated."

"Because I know how I feel about you. And I know wherever you are is where I want to be. The universe wants us to be together, remember?"

I felt my heart begin to race. It was time to do what I came to do. I reached deep within my pants pocket and was relieved to feel the coolness of the tiny gold band. I slid it onto the tip of my finger and brought it into the light. Sunbeams played off the water and danced among the leaves, making the diamond glisten. Over the sound of the falls, I heard Brooke draw in her breath.

"Oh, Charlie," she whispered.

After all we had been through together; the timelines lived and relived, the timelines lost to us, the deaths we mourned and the ones we simply moved on from, the love and friendship that persevered through it all, it was time to make good on a promise I made during a timeline only Brooke remembered.

"You told me once that I promised to wait for you when you broke up with me after Branson got sick. I don't remember it, of course, but it sounds like something I would say." I took her hands in mine. "I want you to know, in this time, in this place, I will always wait for you. I will always love you. I will always need you more than you need me. And I will always drag you on bug-infested hikes when you least expect it. Brooke, my amazing, wonderful Brooke, when I asked you before, I never got my answer, so I'm asking you again today... will you marry me?"

She didn't move or even consider the ring, but instead looked directly into my eyes. I could see it inside of her, the old soul she carried around. I hoped it wasn't so old that it would cause her to hesitate or second guess how she felt about me. Or more so, how she felt about us. But instead of squealing or carrying on the way some women do when presented with a marriage proposal, she reacted as she always did to serious matters. She spoke from her heart.

"Each time I lost Branson, parts of me died. Loving you brought those parts back to life." She closed her eyes and breathed deeply. "I don't think I could say no to you even if I wanted to, because you're right... the universe wants us to be as one. It just keeps bringing us back together, over and over again. I think if I said no, it would just find a way to lead me to you all over again."

I suddenly realized I was trembling. "Do you want to say no?"

She held out her hand. She was shaking too. "I'd say yes to you in a million timelines if I had to, just to be sure we got it right."

I slid the ring on her finger, and she sank into my arms.

"Let's just stick with this timeline, okay?" I asked, holding her close.

"You got it."

Brooke curled up against my chest and gazed at the ring on her finger. As we sat together, laughing and talking and swatting bugs, I reflected upon who I'd always been and who I was about to become. It was hard to believe how desperately I'd tried to discover who I was by looking backward, when all along, all I really needed to do was look to the future. My future was with Brooke, and I knew I'd never question my place in the world again.

Aknowledgements

To the adopted children and adults, and each of the family members I had the privilege of speaking to regarding your own personal journeys, thank you from the bottom of my heart for bearing your souls to me and giving me a glimpse into what it's like to be adopted. I hope Charlie's story speaks for you in some small way.

To my amazing editor Anne, thank you for plowing through rewrite after rewrite with me. Thank you for not sparing my feelings, for rolling your eyes at me when necessary, and for knowing the proper use of hyphens. And also, thanks for being my friend.

To everyone who asked for a sequel to The Clay Lion and who kept checking in to find out when Tin Men would be done, thank you for giving me a reason to keep writing. And for making me feel treasured.

And finally, to my amazing husband and kids who encourage me to keep doing what I love for the simple joy of doing it... thank you. You're the best.

CPSIA information can be obtained at www.ICGtesting.com
Printed in the USA
LVOW10s2048160115

423165LV00009B/175/P